TOD GOLDBERG

is the author of the novels *Living Dead Girl*, a
finalist for the *Los Angeles Times* Book Prize, and
Fake Liar Cheat. A two-time winner of the
Nevada Press Association Prize for his long-
running weekly column in the *Las Vegas Mercury*,
Tod Goldberg lives in La Quinta, CA with his
wife Wendy and teaches creative writing for the
UCLA Extension Writers' Program. Visit him
online at TodGoldberg.com.

SIMPLIFY

STORIES

TOD GOLDBERG

OV BOOKS

an imprint of
Other Voices
magazine

Chicago, Illinois

ALSO BY TOD GOLDBERG

Living Dead Girl
Fake Liar Cheat

For Tom Filer, who took me in and showed me how;
And for Wendy, who gave me the words.

These stories originally appeared, often in significantly different form, in the following publications: "The Jesus of Cathedral City" in the *Santa Monica Review*, "Simplify" and "Comeback Special" in *Other Voices*, "The Living End" in *The Sun*, "The Last Time We Never Met" in *Vortical Magazine*, "Try Not To Lose Her" in *West Wind Review*, "Love Somebody" in *Timber Creek Review*, "Disappear Me" in *Indigenous Fiction*, "The Distance Between Us" in *Pedestal Magazine*.

Library of Congress Cataloging-in-Publication Data

Goldberg, Tod.
    Simplify : stories / Tod Goldberg.
        p. cm.
    ISBN 0-9767177-0-0 (cloth) -- ISBN 0-9767177-1-9 (pbk.)
    I. Title.
    PS3557.O35836S56 2005
    813'.6--dc22

        2005012855

Cover photograph:
And Sally Makes Three © Ned & Shiva Productions

Book design by Lee Nagan,
Fisheye Graphic Services, Inc., Chicago

Printed in the United States of America

www.othervoicesmagazine.org

What a chimera then is man!
What a novelty! What a monster,
what a chaos, what a contradiction,
what a prodigy!

— Blaise Pascal, *Pensees*

CONTENTS

THE JESUS OF CATHEDRAL CITY

We wake up early, before dawn, and dress in the dark. Pam washes her face and brushes her teeth slowly, then wipes her mouth and eyes with a soft white towel. I sit on the bed and watch her; the way she moves automatically every morning, the way she stares at herself in the mirror like she's trying to find something, like she's lost a thought somewhere and if she looks hard enough it will come back, will fly out through the mirror and back into her mind.

"I love you," I say. "I don't know if I say that enough."

Pam smiles at me in the mirror. "Do you like my hair?" she asks. "Do you think it's flattering to my face?"

"Yes," I say.

"All right," she says. "Then I love you, too."

We walk outside to the front porch and lace up our running shoes. The air is cold and wet and I think that tomorrow when we run our breath will stay in the air, will hover between us like a ghost, and maybe Pam will make a joke about Christmas being around the corner and what would I like this year? What can Santa bring her husband? What she'll mean, what she'll be saying beneath all her words, is: Will He come back this year? Do you think He'll find us again?

"It's getting cold," Pam says.

"Maybe it will frost over tomorrow," I say.

Pam nods her head and then blows into her hands, warming them. "How far do you want to run today?" she asks.

"I've got time for a mile," I say.

"I might keep going," she says. "You know they run a 10K here after Thanksgiving. Maybe we can get in shape and do that."

"Maybe," I say, and we're off.

Two years ago, I found Him at a Toys-R-Us in Walnut Creek, California. The year before, inside a bar in Portland, Oregon, where I'd gone to apply for a job waiting tables. He never looks the same, not to me anyway, but I always know it's Him.

The first time, five years ago, was in Cathedral City, a town just outside of Palm Springs, where Pam and I had come for our first wedding anniversary. He was walking down the street during the annual Christmas Gay Pride Cavalcade wearing a dress that made Him look like Scarlett O'Hara.

"Look at that guy," Pam said. "He's got the spirit!"

He turned then and looked directly at us. Even from across the street, His eyes were dark blue, like sapphires, and I found myself trying to catch my breath, trying to hold back tears, and failing. Pam fell to one knee and started sputtering, her voice coming out in hoarse rasps of words, sounds, prayers.

He knifed across the crowded street, sliding between floats and cars and people, His eyes never wavering, until He was standing directly in front of us.

"You can see me?" He said.

"Yes," I said.

"Unreal," He said, not like kids say it, but as if that's what it was, unreal. "What am I wearing?"

"A dress," I said.

"Like *Gone With the Wind*?"

"Exactly," I said.

He knelt down so that He was eye level with Pam. He put a hand on her wrist and she stopped crying. "It's okay," He said. "Can you speak?"

"Yes," Pam said, but her voice was near a whisper.

"Do I have a beard?"

"No," Pam said. "You're too young." He was improbably young, like a teenager, but His hair was flecked with gray.

He nodded carefully. "That's important," He said. "Good. And you can both see me? Incredible."

"Are you Jesus?" I said, which sounded amazing to me.

He shrugged. "I am that I am," He said.

We run alongside the river for a time and then peel off toward downtown Reno. I've gotten fat in the last few years. Pam says it's normal for a man of thirty-five to gain weight. But I've found myself expanding in the damndest places: behind my knees, along the back of my neck, the folds of my fingers. In the last year, I've gained over one hundred pounds. What's amazing is that every doctor I've gone to says that I am healthy and fit, that my heart is in immaculate shape, and that my lungs are as clean as the day I was born. It's a miracle, they say.

We stop in front of the Cal Neva Hotel, where I work in the coffee shop. Pam glistens with sweat but doesn't look tired. She's like a horse now, can run for hours without stopping. "Are you just going to wash up here?" she says.

"I think so," I say. "Is that all right? Are you okay to be alone?"

"I'm fine," she says.

We stare at each other for a moment, and before I know it we are both laughing.

"I think it's about time," I say. "I think He'll probably roll through sometime today."

"What will He be this time?" Pam says.

"I don't know," I say. "I'm not hedging my bets this year."

Pam nods her head; she won last year with a guess that He'd be our plumber. She was off by a bit. He actually delivered us a pizza from Domino's, but since He showed up in a uniform Pam was declared the winner.

Three hours earlier, we'd won the California State Lottery, all $18 million of it. It's all still sitting there, unclaimed. We've been tempted to claim it every now and again, like when Visa canceled our credit card or when Pam saw a purse she really liked, but it's not that simple. Temptation is a boundless thing. It creeps up on you when you least want it, when everything seems to be working just as you'd like. We have another month before the money goes back to the State. Sometimes when I can't sleep, I think I should just claim it and set up a college fund for an entire orphanage, or I should walk down skid row handing out twenties. But there are consequences for those actions, too. There's the press who wants to interview you, the people who want to take advantage of your kindness. We just want a simple life. So Pam and I try to stay with each other as much as possible, to stop ourselves from being as human as the next guy. It's not easy. It's damn hard.

"I think He'll be a child," Pam says. "That would be original."

"And seasonal," I say.

A truck rolls past us on the street and the two men sitting in the bed whistle at Pam. She ignores them.

"I wish that would stop," she says. "I hate that. Do you think we could say something about that to Him?"

"No," I say.

"No," Pam says. "I guess not." She leans into me and kisses me once on the nose. "Be safe, all right?"

"I will," I say.

"And I'll keep my eyes open for the serpent," Pam says, and she jogs away, back toward the river.

Pam and I are not religious people, even now. I've never prayed, never really gotten down on my knees and asked God for a favor, and I don't think I'll start now; despite all of this. Pam says she's afraid that if she started praying, someone might actually answer her and that would be a little too much to handle.

In Cathedral City, when He appeared in drag, He said, "This is an important event. You guys understand that, right?"

"I'm not sure," I said. We'd moved off the parade route and

were sitting on benches drinking coffee outside Eveleen's Café. Pam still wasn't really speaking.

"Oh yeah," He said. "This hasn't happened in a long time. What year is this?"

"1999," Pam said, and she sounded surprised, like she couldn't believe she still knew that.

"We're talking lifetimes then," He said.

"Where have you been?" I said.

"Right here," He said. "Everywhere. No one ever recognizes me, though. Sometimes I'm not even visible. It's crazy, isn't it?"

"Yes," I said.

"This isn't real," Pam said. "Is it?"

"Do you want it to be?" He asked.

Pam looked at me, like she wanted me to answer for her, but I didn't know what to say. "Are there responsibilities associated with all of this?" Pam said, finally. "I mean, do we need to worry about anything, or is there going to be, I dunno, something with the devil that we need to watch out for?"

He took a sip from His latte and then closed His eyes. "Are you asking if you'll be expected to do things? No. There's no contract involved here. I'm not expecting you to start spreading the Word. As for the devil," He said, his eyes still closed, "well, that's tricky."

"So it's true?" I said. "About heaven and hell and all that stuff?"

He opened His eyes, shook His head, and took another sip from His coffee. "Yes and no. It's like this latte. You have a certain expectation of what it's going to taste like, past experience and that sort of thing, and when it meets your expectations or exceeds them, it's almost a bonus. But when you get one that's bitter and the milk isn't foamy, you think, well, I should have considered where I was buying it from."

"Are you saying Heaven is a Starbucks?" Pam said.

"Kind of," He said. "What I'm really saying is that it's all about expectations. Can you expect to have some problems with the devil?

Yes. Is there going to be a fellow with a cloven hoof and a bunch of minions chasing you around? Probably not. But I'm sure he's aware of the situation and monitoring it closely."

I wash up in the employee bathroom and towel off in front of the mirror. I used to know how I'd look every day, used to be able to predict within reason whether or not a pair of pants would fit me as they had before, used to be able to look in the mirror and notice nothing, absolutely nothing, out of the ordinary.

Today, I have an ache in my gums, not unlike the day Pam woke up and her breasts were killing her. I open my mouth and examine my teeth. I spread my lips apart and rub my index finger along my front bottom teeth, where the pain is radiating. Just below the skin, straining to break free, is another row of teeth.

"This is not happening," I say, but immediately know that it is. Just like when Pam woke up a 30A and went to bed a 40DD. Jesus, I think, What next?

I call the house and leave a message for Pam on the voice mail. "He's coming today, for sure," I say. "I've got new teeth growing in my mouth, about seven of them."

By the time I've taken and served my first order of steak and eggs, I can already feel the beginnings of a very sharp molar toward the back of my mouth, this time on the top.

In Walnut Creek, He was dressed as Santa. In Portland, He was tending bar at a place called Pearl's Gate. He has a sense of irony, that much I've learned. I've also learned that He cares about Pam and me, not in the way that He loves all of His children, or whatever the saying is, but in that He likes to hang out with us, likes to listen to us talk about our families and our problems, and that He really appreciates a decent cup of coffee.

But that doesn't mean that either of us likes to be involved with Him. The side effects can be devastating. Worried about spending an eternity rotting in Hell? Why not try gaining one hundred pounds in a year, or developing very large breasts, or winning the lottery, or growing more teeth, or just about anything else Pam and I have suffered through since Jesus became our friend.

He told us it might be like this when we first met Him five years ago.

"It's been great meeting you two," He said. He'd gotten tired of all the noise from the parade and wanted to go downtown to see what was happening, so when a horse-drawn carriage ferrying tourists back to Palm Springs came by, He flagged it down. He sat facing Pam and me so that He could alert us to points of local interest. "I never have anyone who wants to go around in one of these things anymore. Everyone is always so concerned with getting to and from places in the least amount of time. We just passed Lawrence Welk's old house, by the way."

Pam turned back and looked. "Wasn't that Liberace's old house?"

"Oh," He said. "Right. I get these things wrong sometimes. I'm not really sure who either of them are, or were. Just landmarks, something to show tourists when they come to town. I like to be a good host at least, wherever I am."

"You've been wonderful," Pam said, and when it looked like she might cry again, He reached over and patted her knee.

"It's all right," He said. "No need for sadness now. We're just having fun."

"Will we see you again?" I said.

"I wanted to talk about that," He said. "Things are going to be different now. I can't tell you precisely how, because it generally varies from case to case, and it's been years since I've had this kind of connection, but you can expect to encounter a few unpleasant things alongside some really great things, which are also terribly unpleasant, and then some remarkable things that may seem terrible but will end up seeming miraculous. And, from time to time, I expect that the three of us will run into each other when the moment is right, or when I'm really needed, or when I really need you guys."

"This doesn't sound good," I said. "You're scaring me."

Jesus grimaced. "I know," He said. "It never comes out right."

At noon, after my manager informs me that customers are getting a little freaked out by the amount of blood and, well, *teeth* I have in my mouth and couldn't I use some time off to see a dentist, Pam comes and takes me home.

"This is a real mess," Pam says. "I brought some cotton balls. Do you want to put them in your mouth?"

"Cotton makes me gag," I say.

"Are you in pain?"

"Pam," I say, "I have an extra row of teeth in my mouth! Of course I'm in pain."

"Okay," she says. "I'm sorry. I'm just, I don't know, trying to figure out how this all ties together. Do you want to go to the dentist?"

"We don't have any insurance yet," I say. "And any dentist who sees this is going to immediately call another dentist and by eleven o'clock tonight there will be camera crews and the *National Enquirer* sitting in front of our house. Do you want that?"

"Maybe it will make Him come sooner," Pam says. "He can fix this."

I don't say anything because I'm thinking about how many times I've thought He could help us, how He might be able to throw some biblical perspective on things, but it all boils down to what He told us right before we shook hands and left each other in Palm Springs.

"You're chosen people," He said. "For whatever that's worth, it's true."

"I'd like a better job," I said. "Will this help?"

"I'm not a genie," He said. "I'm just the Son of God."

Pam fixes me some soup and then the two of us sit on the couch and wait for something to happen. Usually, when something cataclysmic happens to one of us, like the day Pam's breasts grew ten sizes, the devil makes himself known. Here's what Pam and I have learned about the devil: it's a lot like having your fourteen-year-old nephew around all the time. He's mischievous, sloppy, and occasionally mean. Not scary-Jeffrey-Dahmer-style mean, more like the kids at the mall who throw their gum at senior citizens.

Like the day we won the lottery. Neither one of us had bought a ticket. Instead, as we sat watching the news on the Wednesday before Thanksgiving, it came floating in through an open window. Then, right when the Lotto numbers flashed on the TV screen, the ticket fluttered down, face up, onto Pam's lap.

"Don't look at it," I said, but Pam had already picked it up.

"It's not like it will turn me to stone," Pam said.

"Again," the newscaster said, "today's winning Lotto numbers are 6, 12, 18, 24, 30, and 36. Look at that, Connie, they're all multiples of six. I wonder what the statistical odds of that are?"

Before Connie could answer, Pam and I were already upstairs looking for our suitcases and making guesses as to how He'd appear. Just like right now, with my mouth full of teeth and a bowl of soup in front of me.

"Maybe He'll be a dentist," Pam says.

"Funny," I say. She's trying to make me feel better. It's not working. "Do we have any Advil? I feel like I've got nails in my gums."

"We could go to the store," Pam says, but then thinks better of it. "I guess you should probably stay inside."

Every time something happens to Pam and me, the world shrinks. In Walnut Creek, when He appeared as Santa, I saved a family of four who were pinned beneath their overturned minivan. I just lifted it right off of them, like I was Superman. In Portland, when He was working at the bar, Pam brushed against a blind woman in Powell's bookstore. The woman dropped to her knees and began shouting, "I can see! I can see!"

It's a curse. Sometimes, we believe it is Him at work; other times we are certain it is the devil. We could profit from this life, could become stars, figures in history even, but neither of us has asked for this. Instead, we've become transients, never staying in one place for more than a year. It becomes difficult to stay anonymous, to succeed when others are toiling, and to avoid the hand of temptation, good and bad. And to dodge being stared at when the remarkable occurs. People notice these things.

Pam looks at her watch and then gets up to take a peek outside. "I could run down to Safeway by myself, but I'm a little worried about leaving you," she says. "What if the other guy shows up?" She never calls the devil "The Devil." She refuses to concede that he even exists; instead she likens his existence to that of the Yeti, or the Loch Ness monster. Something many people believe in, but none have any concrete proof of. Pam is an optimist. Even when we've seen the devil, Pam has refused to acknowledge him. Never even says hello. I try to be pleasant, just in case. She says if she doesn't speak to him she can rationalize all of this away. I love Pam, I really do.

"I'll be fine," I say. "Maybe get some beer and a pound of Starbucks coffee. It could be a long night."

The devil is a beer drinker. He likes Beck's.

"If you think so," Pam says. "I'll get a six-pack of Milwaukee's Best, just in case."

The first time we actually saw the devil was shortly after we ran into Jesus in Cathedral City. We'd said our goodbyes with Jesus and while He promised to contact us every now and again, both Pam and I were more than a touch skeptical. What had we really seen? Had we really met the Son of God? Why was he dressed like Scarlett O'Hara? Why us? What now?

We went back to our hotel room and watched Pay-Per-View movies all night, neither one of us sure of what to say to the other. After Pam fell asleep, I crawled out of bed and walked downstairs to the lobby bar and had a glass of chardonnay in hopes it might calm me down.

I sat there for a time sipping my wine and watching the scores flutter by on ESPN. I thought about all the times in my life when I'd said His name in vain, thought about the silent prayers I'd made for sorority girls, open freeways, and the Oakland Athletics. What if I'd hallucinated? What if Pam and I both had eaten something really bad at dinner and all of this was just a figment of our imaginations? But then I realized that in order to have any of these thoughts, to be cognizant of all of these questions, all of this *had to have happened.*

"What are you drinking, sport?"

To my right was a man dressed in an immaculate linen suit. He had a head of full blond hair and a thick mustache. He smelled like baby powder and apples.

"I'm sorry," I said. "I just want to be alone."

"No problem here," he said. "First time in the desert?"

"I'm not trying to be rude," I said, "but when I said I wanted to be left alone, I really meant it."

"No offense taken," he said. "How's Pam taking this?"

I almost answered him. I almost just said that, hey, both of us are feeling pretty winded by this whole deal and thanks for asking. But I stopped myself. I actually put my hand over my mouth and shook my head so that I could clear the words. The man in the linen suit frowned at me and then waved the bartender over.

"Another chardonnay here for my boy," he said, "and a foreign beer for me. Something German if you have it."

"How did you know my wife's name?" I asked.

"You must have mentioned it," he said. "Yes, you said that you and she had a rather bad hallucination from some rancid food at dinner."

"I didn't say that," I said.

"Didn't you?" he said. "I thought I heard that."

It was possible, I thought. Sure. I could have said that out loud. Except that I knew I hadn't. "No, no, no," I said. "Don't buy me a drink. I don't want anything from you."

"We don't even know each other," he said. "You don't even know my name."

"You're the other guy," I said.

"That's a matter of perspective—I know quite a few people who think I'm the only guy." The man in linen flicked something off the lapel of his suit. The bartender set down another glass of wine and a bottle of beer. "Ah, Beck's! Thank you, barkeep, one thousand thank you's!"

I stood up and dropped a twenty on the bar. "I'd love to stick around," I said, "but none of this is happening and, even if it were, I'd rather it happen with Pam here."

"She's coming down right now," he said. "She's looking for you."

Just then, Pam rounded the corner into the bar, clad only in her underwear and a tank top. The man in the linen suit started giggling like a five-year-old.

"Pam," I said. "What are you doing?"

"I don't know," she said. "I had a dream that you and the devil were having drinks in the lobby bar and the next thing I know I'm here. Is this happening? Am I standing here in my underwear?"

The man in the linen suit got up, pocketed my twenty, and started to make his way out of the bar.

"Hey," I said. "What the hell do you think you're doing?"

He turned and gave a little bow. "Just introducing myself," he said. "Get you familiar with how I work. A real pleasure meeting you and your wife. She has lovely sleep clothes."

"Bastard," I said.

"The first," he said.

Pam calls me from the grocery store on her cell phone.

"Honey," I say, "stop crying. I can't understand you."

"It's so stupid," she says. "I should be used to this by now. Five years, you'd think I could control myself."

Pam is doing what she always does when she sees Him; no matter how He appears, Pam falls to the ground and starts blubbering.

"It's okay," I say. "Is He coming over?"

"Later," Pam manages through sniffles. "His shift at the store isn't over for another hour."

"He's a checker at Safeway?"

"He's gathering the stray carts in the parking lot," Pam says, "and helping people carry their groceries out."

Before we hang up, I tell Pam to pick up some packing tape and a box of green garbage bags in case we need to get out of town in a hurry.

"I don't want to leave anymore," Pam says. "I just want to live. Don't you?"

"I do," I say, and I tell her that I love her and to get home soon.

There are times in your life when you accept things for what they are. Though Pam and I have done just that, it doesn't make any of this easier; Pam wants a family and so do I. The obstacles seem too large to hurdle: do I want to bring a child into a life where the choices of good and evil visit on a regular basis? Pam doesn't say it like that—she just worries about *Rosemary's Baby* coming true.

When Pam gets home from the store, she's still a little shaken. We go upstairs and lie down on the bed, so that we can hug each other and talk about our options. It's come to the point that neither of us wants to lose Jesus, but we can't imagine living like this anymore.

"We'll just tell Him that he needs to work something out with the other guy," I say. "Get everyone to stop bothering us. Do you think that will work?"

"I don't know," Pam says. "We do some good things for people. Who picks up the slack?"

"We're not responsible for the human race, Pam," I say. "I have a hard enough time waiting tables. I mean, look at us. Remember when our bodies were our bodies? Not some battleground? Remember when we could be tempted to do something stupid or selfish? I miss that. I miss not knowing about the world. Don't you?"

"We've been blessed," Pam says quietly.

He's wearing baggy black jeans and a ripped T-shirt that hangs off His body like swaddling. His arms are thick and muscled and a tattoo that says JESUS SAVES in Old English wraps around His left bicep. He has a skinny goatee and His hair is cropped close to his head.

And He's standing on my front porch holding an espresso machine.

"Can I come inside?" He asks, His voice tinged with excitement. "I've just learned how to fix a latte."

"Of course," I say.

He looks at me and frowns. "Oh boy," He says. "What's going on in your mouth?"

"I'm growing teeth," I say. "It's not a real pleasant experience."

"I'm sorry," He says, and He touches my arm. A wave passes through me; it feels like water and air and Christmas morning when I was eleven. The pain in my mouth evaporates. "Is that better?"

"Thank you," I say.

After He sets His espresso machine up and starts brewing lattes, Jesus comes and sits with Pam and me in the living room. He looks tired, which is odd. He always appears full of life.

"We want to talk to you about something," I say. "If you are up for it."

He raises His eyebrows in surprise. "I'm always up for it," He says. "You should know that."

"You look tired," Pam says. "Are you all right?"

He smiles then in a way that makes me want to cry, but I don't. "I haven't been all right for a very long time," He says. "That's how I exist. But it serves me well, keeps me on my toes."

"Look," I say, and Pam puts her hand over mine and gives it

a little squeeze. "This has become too much for us. We want to have a family and to live in one place, you know? Set some kind of roots. We're afraid of becoming a spectacle."

"Tabloid messiahs," He says. "Am I on the right track?"

"Exactly," Pam says.

"We just want to have a clear-cut life," I say. "We want to make mistakes and have temptation."

"I can understand that," He says.

"We don't want to lose You," Pam says. "But we also don't want to go to church and become zealots. We just want to know that we can go on without all the side effects and without worrying about where we go, you know, *afterward*."

"Pam," He says, "Blessed are the poor in spirit and the pure of heart."

"I don't know what that means," Pam says.

"Me either," I say.

"Don't either of you read?" He says. When we don't respond, He lowers His voice and says, "You've always got a place to live. Don't worry."

"I guess we're both concerned about the other guy," I say.

Jesus stands up abruptly. "For that, we'll definitely need more coffee," He says, and then scuttles off to the kitchen.

We talk for hours about our fears, our lives, our expectations. He's big on expectations. He says it helps determine a lot.

"We will both always be here," He says about the devil. "Here and now aren't really all that important. It's transitive, but you don't need to know that. Your expectation is that if you keep on being pulled by him and Me that eventually you'll just break. Am I right?"

"Yes," I say. "And I, at least, feel that literally in light of my teeth and all."

"Right," He says. "And to some degree you are correct. Both of you have been used for different purposes and the effects are physical. You've been peacemakers, which I appreciate, and you've saved some people, which I always think is great. I guess it comes down to deciding if you want to stop being special."

"I don't like feeling like an instrument," Pam says.

"No," He says, nodding. "I suppose not."

"Will the other guy bother us?" I ask.

"Yes," He says. "No matter what happens, you will be ruled by temptation. I can't change that. It's how you lead your life that matters. But I understand that you want a life and I can give you that."

"All right," I say.

"Yes," Pam says. "We'd like that."

"Poof," He says. "That was easy."

"That's it?" I say. My mouth is still full of teeth. I'm still fat. Pam is still big breasted. Jesus is still sitting in my living room wearing baggy pants and a torn shirt.

"I don't use *mirrors*," He says. "It comes down to choice. You're free to walk this earth as you always have, free to make mistakes and be kind to people and to ignore people and maybe every now and again you'll help someone who needs helping. And that will be fine. Maybe you'll see something violent and you'll think you could have prevented it, and maybe you'll be right, but maybe you would have died in the process. It's all in the choices, the details. You're both free to do whatever you want to do. Now, let's see about learning how to make Frappuccino. Who wants one?"

We live our life in blindness now and it suits both of us. It's how these things are supposed to end, these miracles, these twists of fate and time. How else could it possibly be? I believe in devotion and hope now, believe that all things are possible and impossible. Which leads to this: Pam is pregnant. Her belly is round and soft and at night I pray that our child is safe from harm, pray that I can provide for my family, and that I am able to keep away from temptation, both pleasant and dreadful.

We've seen Jesus twice since we told Him we wanted different lives. The first time was on TV, answering phones during a pledge drive on PBS. He appeared to be in His mid-thirties and He was wearing a baseball cap that read JOHN 3:16. The last time was today.

They sat facing each other in the park where we used to jog but now only walk, a chessboard between them, bickering. Jesus was a dapper old man with a thin Clark Gable mustache. He was wearing a red cardigan, tan chinos, and a pair of sharp penny loafers. The devil, resplendent in fine linen from head to toe, looked about the same age.

"We should go," Pam said, her eyes beginning to tear up.

"They don't see us," I whispered. "Can't we watch them for a second?"

"Only for a second," Pam said. We crept behind a row of junipers and sat down. The sun was out and the air was warm and alive with the sounds of their voices.

"I will not have this argument with you," Jesus said. "We play for sport only."

"Always so stuffy, old chap," the devil said. "Always rules about everything. Why not raise the stakes? Give the game some meaning!"

"Raise the stakes?" Jesus said. "I win and you give back temptation. How's that?"

"Fine," the devil said. "And you, old chap, should I win, give me Heaven."

"Agreed," Jesus said.

Before either of us were able to jump out to scream our objections, both men burst into laughter.

"A beautiful day for a game of chess," Jesus said, after His laughter had finally subsided, and then He began to assemble His pieces.

"Indeed," the devil said. "A wonderful day."

SIMPLIFY

I am in The Contraption. My eyes, which the doctor has dilated, are pinned open. Dad sits behind me, in the dark, tapping his foot on the floor. The chart is the only thing illuminated in the room. My eyes are getting so dry, I can feel them shriveling up; they will roll down my cheek any minute now and bounce across the cool floor. I know this will happen. They are getting very dry.

The eye doctor tells me to read the letters. "Little b. Little b. Little b." He flips something on The Contraption, and I read again. "Little d. Little d. Little d." There is not much time left until my eyes turn into raisins and drop from their sockets.

"Again," he says. This time there are numbers. "Seven. Seven. One. Seven." I hear my father cough, like he does before he goes on the air. My dad is The Voice of the City on Channel 2. He uses a fake voice when he does the news. He always coughs before he does it. Tonight he'll tell all of the Bay Area that his son's eyes shriveled up like raisins and fell out of their dry sockets. "Wall Street climbed twenty-five points in heavy trading," he'll say, and that will be that.

"Okay, chief," the eye doctor says. "One more chart and then I'll give you some 3-D glasses. You like 3-D, don't you?"

I don't say anything because the time is now. If I move my mouth they will fall. I can't afford to move a muscle. He places a new chart in front of my eyes, my raisin eyes that will soon be my glass eyes, and tells me to read. "Big D. Big D. Big D. Big L. Big L." My father coughs again, like he did before he told everyone about the President resigning.

"One more," the eye doctor says, but I can't take it. I begin to scream "Raisins!" because I think that's all I've got left: two dried-up black raisins. I scream until my dad finally tells the doctor to get me out of the damn Contraption before I burst a blood vessel.

"Dyslexia," the eye doctor says, "is manageable." I search for a hidden toaster in *Highlights Magazine* but can't find it because my eyes are dilated and I'm wearing 3-D glasses.

Third grade and I'm in a class for retards. There is Natalie Hash who has two plastic arms with mechanical hooks on them. She tells me that she was run over by a steamroller and kisses my ear until I wet myself a little and push her away. Joe O'Neil stutters and blinks. I stay away from him. Kirk Hartman, Natalie tells me, has a vagina. I don't believe her. I feel out of place.

Mrs. Blass is our teacher, and she's very nice. She has long black hair with streaks of blond. I tell her that her hair looks like a picture of the Milky Way I have on my wall. I tell her that my dad met Neil Armstrong and that one day I will be an astronaut. She smiles at me and pats my head like Dad pats our dog. It makes me feel pretty good.

I exercise every day with Kirk Hartman. We walk on balance beams, we throw a tennis ball off a wall, and we learn to write the "new" alphabet. This seems dumb to me because I've been writing it differently for two years without a problem. But Mrs. Blass tells me I need to learn the right way. She pats my head, and when she is just out of hearing range, I give her a little bark. Kirk laughs, but I hit him on the arm and tell him not to hear me.

I keep the "old" alphabet in my head because I think it works better. The letters mean more to me than the new ones do. Since I am forbidden to use it at school, I use my alphabet for other things. I change the shape of some letters, sawing off the rough edges here and there, curling loops around others. Some letters get assigned to people. My favorite letter is X, so I give it to Mrs. Blass. Except I change it to look like a ballerina doing a pirouette and color it black and gold to match Mrs. Blass's hair. The problem is I can't draw it like I see it. It ends up looking like a nine. I assign my sister Kelly the letter R, but I flip it upside down and put a star on either side of it.

After school, I always walk home with my sister Kelly. She is two years older than me. We throw rocks at each other while we walk, and sometimes we stop and spit on bugs. We get along better at home than on the way there. Kelly is very smart. She is in advanced math and is already learning pre-algebra. She wears a calculator-watch. I'm not real confident with time yet.

Mom is very active in the community, so there are days when we come home and she's not there. She says she has civic responsibilities because Dad is The Voice of the City. When Mom is not home I feel nervous. I worry that Kelly will choke on beef jerky, or our dog will have puppies and I won't know what to do. I spend a lot of time in my room looking at the maps of space Dad gave me on my birthday. Neil Armstrong told my dad that NASA is always looking for good astronauts.

Dad doesn't spend much time at home. He anchors the news at 6:00 and 11:00. He also makes documentaries. He did one about stewardesses that won him an Emmy for local broadcasting. He is a very important man, my mom says.

One day I hear my dad tell my mom that he deserves everything he's got. That he's worked damn hard to give us all a home and something he calls "creature comforts." I am sitting in the family room playing with my army men, arranging them in the creases and folds of an old comforter. Dad lights a cigarette and sits down on the couch across from me. He watches me arrange the men for a battle I will wage silently. I prefer to set the men up and then just look at them, imagining bullets ripping through their plastic bodies, heads spinning wildly down the seams of the comforter. Each of the two hundred men has a name, but as a group they are the letter Q. There is little in the way of modification to that letter, because it is a very sinister-looking letter. It is slithery and mean.

"Ray," my dad says. "Before your sister gets back, I want to have a man-to-man chat." He flattens a pillow on the couch that he wants me to sit on. I allow five men to die before I take my place next to him. "Son," he says, and I let a helicopter drop a bomb on a small village of Kelly's Barbie dolls. "I've been offered a wonderful opportunity to work for the network in Los Angeles. So next week I'm going to move down there and start looking for a new house for all of us. You and Kelly and your mother will stay here until the end of the school year." I fix my eyes on my father's left foot, which has just swept over the heads of Alfred and Nick the Stick; their screams echo in my head. They were good soldiers. "What do you think about all of this?" my dad asks.

"I think it's fine," I say. "You've got all you've deserved."

My dad gives me a strange look and then puts his arm around me and squeezes me tight. "You're going to be the biggest little man in the house," he says, and kisses my head. Two more men die when a recon mission comes under heavy enemy fire.

My dad and mom become the letter Y.

I tell my classmates that my father is moving away to become an astronaut. Natalie tells me that her arms are made from the same materials that NASA uses and then tries to kiss me on the lips. I bite her chin and draw blood. It tastes salty and warm, not unlike the sauce for French Dip. Mrs. Blass yanks me into the bathroom and makes me wash my mouth out with soap. She is beautiful, and I tell her that she moves like a ballerina and that she is X.

At a parent-teacher-student conference the next day, Mrs. Blass tells my mom that she can't help me anymore, that I'm smart enough to do anything I want, but there is a problem about application. She says that again: "Application." While they talk, I draw a picture of Mrs. Blass spinning on her tiptoes; her arm is arched up and the colors are perfect. I slide the picture across Mrs. Blass's desk and she picks it up.

"Do you see what I mean?" she says to my mom. My mom smiles and takes my hand in hers.

When we get home, Mom tells Kelly and me to write a letter to our father. I write mine in the old alphabet and seal it in an envelope before Mom can read it.

Three days later, Dad and Mom have a fight on the phone. I listen on the extension in the family room.

"You've gotta see this, honey," he says. "It's almost like an alien wrote it. There are parts that look like the alphabet, but they are all backwards and twisted up."

"He's very confused is all," she says. "You should have seen the people in his class. It's a wonder he's not worse. His best friend, a boy named Kirk Hartman, is a hermaphrodite of all things."

"I think maybe we should take him to a therapist."

"He's not crazy," she says.

I am moved to a new classroom where the kids are not retarded, but I am singled out because I used to be. Two boys, Scott Sorensen and Phil Miglino, pin me down during recess and write RETARD on my forehead with a thick black marker that smells like licorice. A girl named Hollis, who has buck teeth and stringy hair, tells me she is going to marry me, and then runs off making gagging noises. I miss Mrs. Blass and my exercises with Kirk.

I make friends with a very fat boy named Jamie Smith. He vomits on his desk the second day I am in class, which makes me feel a little less focused-on. I go to his house after school to play.

We sit upstairs in his room and color pictures on large pieces of poster board. He draws Godzilla attacking a boat in the middle of the sea. I tell him that no matter how tall Godzilla might be, he absolutely could not stand up in the deepest parts of the Atlantic Ocean. Jamie responds by ripping up my sketch of the Apollo landing on the moon. Ten minutes later we are friends again.

Jamie and I spend a lot of time at the Quick Stop buying

Slurpees and CornNuts. One afternoon, we see Kirk Hartman there playing pinball.

"He has a vagina," I tell Jamie, though I'm not sure I believe that.

"Do you want to kick his ass?" Jamie asks.

"Sure," I say.

Jamie grabs Kirk by his collar and yanks him out to the street where our bikes are parked. Kirk looks at me like I'm crazy, but all I can do is laugh. We drag Kirk down a rocky gully behind the Quick Stop and then tie his hands behind his back with my bicycle chain and lock. Jamie punches him a couple of times in the face and then tells me to pull off Kirk's pants so that he can see if Kirk has a vagina.

"Ray," Kirk says, but it comes out sounding funny because Jamie has knocked out his two front teeth. "Ray," Kirk says again, but I pull off his pants anyway. He has a penis. Jamie pushes me aside and lifts up Kirk's penis, and then I see it. A vagina, just like Natalie Hash said. Jamie laughs and then brings his knee into Kirk. I look down and Kirk is staring right at me. I turn and run back up the gully, get on my bike and ride home.

At six o'clock that night, Van Humber, the new Voice of the City, announces that a young boy has been found beaten to death behind a Quick Stop in Concord. I hide in my bedroom and listen for police sirens. I listen to every sound the house makes, breaking each noise into parts. The refrigerator is Click-Hiss-Click. The phone is a scream of even pitch. My mother's phone conversation floats into my room. I take apart the words she speaks, breaking them down by sound until they are nothing but grunts. I visualize each letter in every word melting into slush.

Kirk Hartman is O. I take that letter out of my alphabet and vow to never touch it again.

We move to Los Angeles the day after school ends. I've made quite a turnaround, my teachers all agree, and it's true. I have won the spelling bee, tested well in math, and am considered a fine artist. The teachers tell my mom that it is good that I stopped being friends with "that Smith boy" and started concentrating in class. But I concentrate because of him. Because at recess he follows me. Because it is all I can do when he stares at me in class. Because I close down and put him into a little tunnel and find something else in my head.

I decide that I will make some changes in Los Angeles. I will make friends with the cool kids and try out for sports. Math will become my new favorite subject. Secretly, I will keep a journal written solely in my own alphabet. By the end of the summer, I've added several new letters to my alphabet and expect to top one hundred by Christmas break.

School comes easy after I tell everyone who my father is. One of my teachers, Mr. Schreiber, tells the class that my father seems very trustworthy on the news. I fall in love with Julie Glass when she tells me that her mother thinks my dad is sexy.

At home, I play with my *Star Wars* action figures when my parents are around. When they aren't looking, I scribble new letters into my journal. One night my parents have a dinner party with a few "big guns from the network," and Kelly and I sit at the kids' table with the other children. I get nervous because we are supposed to eat with the correct fork and I keep forgetting which of the three is correct. My mom's eyes are on me while I am eating, so I dare not mess up. Kelly confides in me before dinner that this whole evening is a "really big deal" and that I shouldn't say anything stupid or start screaming about raisins. She thinks that is pretty funny. We don't have much in common.

Finally, my mom comes over and excuses us from dinner. My stomach hurts, I tell her.

"Honey," Mom says. "You know where the bathroom is. Just spray some air freshener when you're done."

I grab my notebook and sit on the toilet for an hour. I write a letter to Kirk Hartman in my alphabet. I tell him all about Los Angeles, and about my new friends, and about the new math I'm learning where letters and numbers work together. Sometimes, I write, I can't get the equations to stop running through my head. It makes me feel like a robot. I imagine I am the robot from *Lost in Space* and everyone depends on me. I tell Kirk that I am sorry I let him down.

The door opens and a tall man with steel gray hair is standing in front of me, his hands fumbling with his zipper.

"Oh," he says. "You startled me." He leans down and looks into my journal. "What do you have there, a coloring book?"

"No," I say. "I'm writing a letter."

"Well," he says, still staring at my journal. "Would you mind if I squeezed in here for a moment?"

"Sure," I say, and leave the bathroom. My mom is sitting at the kitchen table talking to a woman with hair like Mrs. Blass's.

"Ray," Mom says. "Come in here and meet Mrs. Stone." I walk over and shake Mrs. Stone's hand.

"I am pleased to meet you," I say.

"He's such a little man," Mrs. Stone says. My mom smiles and says something quietly to Mrs. Stone that makes her blush and giggle a bit. I reach up and touch her hair. It is thick and wiry feeling, nothing like how I imagined Mrs. Blass's hair to be. I see my mother's hand reaching for mine, but I've got to feel the blond streak. Will it be soft and warm? I think it will. It isn't. It is grainy and rough. I pull as hard as I can until my dad grabs me; Mrs. Stone is shrieking and her hair is on the kitchen floor.

We go every Tuesday to see Dr. Lupus for "behavior modification." For the first half hour, either my mom or my dad sits with me and the doctor, and we discuss how to be a better person, how to do the right things, how to know when we are "getting close to that scary place." "That scary place" is mine alone, according to Dr. Lupus. I must learn how to control my desires, he says, and act like a good young man.

The second half hour, Dr. Lupus and I just talk. One day, I decide to give him something to write about.

"I have my own alphabet," I say.

Dr. Lupus stops scribbling. "Really?"

"And I witnessed a murder."

Dr. Lupus sets his journal down and pulls his chair closer to mine. He looks frustrated. "You see, Raymond, this is exactly what we are trying to work on," he says. "We all know how creative and smart you are. You don't need to create scenarios to shock people. Just concentrate on being yourself. Simplify things."

"All right," I say.

My dad changes his name to Nick and gets hired by CNN as a correspondent. He becomes known for going places no one else will. He breaks stories in places like Kuala Lumpur, United Arab Emirates, Libya, Somalia, and El Salvador.

I coast through grade school and middle school because I am popular and smart. The teachers want me in their classes, to use as a good example for others. I try out for sports and sometimes I do well. I can swim the backstroke very quickly. Math makes me the envy of other students because I develop a series of body twitches for multiple-choice exams. The teachers think I get nervous at test time, but I'm just giving out answers. My school gets an award for testing extremely high in state-run math exams, thanks to me.

Kelly learns to drive when I am in the eighth grade. She takes me and two of her friends to school every day. One of her friends, Misty Lawler, sits in the back seat with me. She wears short skirts and lets me touch her underwear. She becomes—by my official count—letter number 489, which resembles an isosceles triangle and an obtuse triangle intersecting one another. Geometry is my new specialty.

I get a letter from Jamie Smith the last day of ninth grade. He tells me he's found Jesus. He tells me that one day very soon he will tell the world that I killed Kirk Hartman. He tells me that Jesus came to him in a dream after he'd smoked some really good weed, and that Jesus told him to recant. He tells me that Kirk Hartman has been seen as a mist, appearing for just a moment then dispersing, behind the Quick Stop, which, he says, is now a Pizza Hut.

I burn the letter.

My dad gets shot in the head by two guerrilla warriors in a jungle just outside of San Salvador. His remains are sent to us in three boxes by the El Salvadoran government. At Dad's funeral, I read a poem that I title "The Voice of the City Will Never Rest." One of his colleagues tells me that I am a very brave boy and a talented writer.

My dad, post-mortem, becomes letters 599 through 612. My mom stays Y, but I alter the letter slightly to reflect the sudden death of my father.

In high school, I become cool. I tell everyone how great the Ramones are, how fluid their simple three-chord progression is, and how much I identify with what they are saying. On my locker I place stickers for bands like the Sex Pistols, The Damned, Generation X, and Discord over every inch of space.

My grades drop dramatically. In order to become cool, I've had to make some sacrifices. I'm following Dr. Lupus's advice. I have no need for history, so I fail it. I have no need for PE, so I fail it. I have some need for English, so I get a D the semester we talk about Chaucer and an A- the semester we focus on current literature. I have a great need for math and score high on the tests. I start tinkering around with computer science.

I become cool by wearing the same outfit every day. Dark blue jeans, with an ironed crease down the center, and a plain white shirt, pressed. On cold days I wear my leather jacket. Kelly tells me I look like a freak. I tell her that I finger-bang Misty Lawler on a regular basis. She tells Mom and now I walk to school.

By the end of tenth grade, I have 845 letters, plus I have added an addendum for people I dislike or am afraid will hurt me.

Jamie Smith becomes the inaugural member when he writes me a second letter.

He writes: *Dear Ray, Jesus is dead. Kirk Hartman is alive. I saw him last week behind the Quick Stop, which was a Pizza Hut, which is now a coffee house called Nectar. Kirk says we should all get together.*

I ask my mom if maybe we shouldn't move to the East Coast so that she can be closer to her parents. "They're not getting any younger," I say. She cries, much as she has every day since my father was used for political purposes, and tells me that I am cruel.

Jamie Smith is my first algebraic formula to be used. He is officially $2(3x + 8)(4x - 2x + 7) = n$. I vow never to solve for n.

Kelly graduates and moves to Seattle to attend the University of Washington. We are friends again because I volunteer to help her pack and because I say that I would love to drive up north with her to keep her safe. She takes me up on the first offer but not the second, which is fine, because it was more of a token suggestion than a real desire.

I attend summer school and make up all my Fs. When I find out that if I continue to let my grades drop I will not graduate, I decide being cool also means not failing out of high school. I still wear my allegiance to punk rock music on my sleeve, but at home I listen to John Coltrane and Otis Redding. They are the only things that stop the numbers and the letters. Under my bed, there are twenty-six notebooks full of alphabet and addenda and letters to my father and Kirk Hartman. I wonder if they know each other. I imagine there are separate heavens for different kinds of death. Maybe people who die violently or under mysterious conditions share a level of heaven. Maybe my dad and Kirk play catch and talk about me. Maybe my dad tells Kirk that I finally kicked that dyslexia thing, but boy, I'm really obsessed with numbers and letters and equations and alphabets.

One night I hear my mom talking to someone on the phone.

"Life will be so much easier when he goes to college," she says. "I've never deserved any of this."

I take the SAT in my junior year, one year early, and score 1480. "That's Ivy League stuff," my guidance counselor says. "You've really buckled down, Ray." I tell him that I owe it all to my belief in power through education. I am wearing a pair of chinos and a light blue Oxford button-down. My hair has grown thick and wavy. I have on Topsiders. I am The Boy You Want Your Daughter To Date. I have removed the punk rock stickers from my locker and replaced them with stickers about world causes. My favorite is ONE PEOPLE, ONE PLANET, PLEASE. Misty Lawler sent it to me from Berkeley. She sprayed a squirt of perfume on it, that, she assured me, contained no animal byproducts.

By the beginning of my senior year, I have sixty-seven notebooks under my bed. I have started writing short stories in my alphabet. I am developing a program on my computer that will be able to read my language.

I come home from school on a Tuesday and my mom is sitting on the floor of my bedroom. All sixty-seven notebooks are scattered on the floor around her. She is crying.

"Ray, what are you?" she says.

"I'm your son," I say, because that is all I can say. In my mind I am running equations. Solve for X. Solve for X. But all I see is Mrs. Blass. How do I solve for X?

My mom lifts up a notebook and there is a drawing of Kirk Hartman and his letter. I have not seen it in years. "Ray, do you know what happened to this boy?"

"Yes," I say. Behind the Quick Stop, which became a Pizza Hut, and then something called Nectar.

"I thought you stopped all this years ago," she says.

"I never stopped," I say. X minus Y equals what?

"Dr. Lupus told me that you'd grow out of this," she says. "That puberty would fix you."

"It's not like I'm torturing animals," I say. The slope of Y equals
mx + b.

"This ends today," my mom says.

"You didn't deserve this," I say and I mean it. I mean my dead
father. I mean me, who will probably end up as a special on the
Discovery Channel. I mean these notebooks filled with an alphabet longer than some languages. I mean the air she breathes, the
food she eats. I mean it all, for a moment.

The last time I use my alphabet is my freshmen year in college.
I've mothballed it for over a year, because I saw how sad it made
my mom. I use it in my head sometimes just to make sure it's still
there, and it is. I can count nearly a thousand letters during a lecture
on revisionist history. But I don't write it down; I don't write letters
to Dad or Kirk in it. I just save it for the times when I feel nervous.

It's the nerves that do me in.

My roommate introduces me to his sister Tina. She is twenty-
two, a junior majoring in Psych, and she thinks that Otis Redding
is God. We have a built-in connection with a man who died too
soon. After our first date, we drive back to her apartment off
campus. I kiss her eyes and her neck. "Wait," she says and gets
up from the bed. She fumbles around in the dark for a minute
and then I hear Otis come through the stereo. Tina is singing along
with him as she crosses the bedroom.

"I've been loving you, for soooo long," she croons. When she
is back on the bed, her top is off. We spend the next two days just
like this.

The next day, I'm walking on campus looking for the vendor
who sells rice bowls. Usually he parks in front of Science II, but
there is a sign saying he is now stationed outside the Psych building. I have a rice bowl every day for lunch, so I trek across campus.

I sit on the grass and eat my rice bowl and watch two squirrels race around the branches of a tree. I feel good about most
everything today. The sun is out. I have my rice bowl. My mom

is in Italy with three girlfriends (according to the postcard). I have spent forty-eight hours experiencing great pleasure. I might rush a fraternity in the winter.

Jamie Smith walks out of the Psych building holding Tina's hand. They stand beneath an awning and she kisses him on the cheek. He takes a step back and smiles. Makes a gesture with his big hands. Frowns like a clown frowns. She kisses him on the lips. He takes the stairs back up inside the building.

My rice bowl spills at my feet. The squirrels pounce. $2(3x + 8) (4x - 2x + 7) = n$.

Tina sees me, frowns like people frown, and starts making a line to me.

I run across campus, through the student union, and all the way to my dorm room.

The walls are blank white and I want to fill them up. I want Tina to know that she has made a tragic mistake, that she has been in bed with a killer. I want Tina to know that there are some emotions you don't play around with, that tenderness is a privilege not a right. I write her a long letter using as many words as I can muster. I access the addendum. I fill the walls with my alphabet. Every last inch of empty wall is filled with my words, my symbols, my algebraic formulas.

When I was a little boy, my dad told me that there are spaces we all fit into. This was when we were driving home from the eye doctor's office. He said that when he was a child he couldn't catch a ball very well, or run very fast, but he could speak. He said, "There are things you can do that don't take great physical skill, Ray. You capitalize on what you do well and then you become what you want."

Maybe Dad had his own alphabet somewhere. Maybe sometimes he couldn't tell if he was seeing a lowercase d or a lowercase b. I've written him a thousand letters—not an official count, because I don't do that anymore—and in each one I apologize for things I've done since he died.

That wasn't Jamie Smith out in front of the Psych building. He's either dead or in prison; I know that now with some certainty. I've never taken the time to solve Jamie's equation—maybe out of fear, maybe out of faith—but I think I'd find the answer to be pretty anti-climatic.

So I live a normal life. I have a wife, a child, a golden retreiver. But sometimes, especially when I watch my son struggle with his first words, I yearn for my alphabet. For the way my mind could twist away for hours assigning, creating, modifying. Compulsion tells me to assign my wife and child a letter, something solitary and distinct that I could base a whole new alphabet on. But I resist. I simplify. I solve for X.

FAITH, LOVE, HOPE

Susie leaves me after three years. Am I ugly? Are my lips too big? What I believe:

Nobody likes me for me. My best quality is probably my car.

I call Dan and ask him to meet me for lunch.

"Can't do it," he says. "Got a real job now."

"What does that mean?"

"No more lunches where we sit around and talk about the future," he says. "My future is in high gear. I don't want you to bring me down."

"Oh," I say.

Dan makes a snorting noise.

"Are we still friends?" I ask.

"Sure," Dan says.

"You know Susie left me."

"No idea," Dan says.

"Yeah," I say.

"All right," Dan says. "I'm gonna let you go."

I sit in Jerry's Deli with a yellow legal pad and prepare to make a list of things I need to change in my life in order to become really happy. While Susie cleaned out her drawers, she was kind enough to land some parting shots in my direction. She told me that nobody thought I was much fun anymore, that even my sister had confided in her that my loyalties have always rested with money and not people, and that, finally, I needed to learn how to give more of myself.

"Fine," I said to Susie. "Why don't we take a vacation. Go to Peru or something."

"See," Susie said, stuffing a handful of socks into a green garbage bag. "You just think you can buy your way out of this. It's not about vacations."

I separate my legal pad into two columns: THINGS I LIKE ABOUT MYSELF and THINGS I DON'T LIKE ABOUT MYSELF.

I attack the positive first:

1. Make wise investments.
2. Sold AOL stock when it hit 120 a share.
3. Don't eat a lot of sweets.
4. Service my car every 3,000 miles.
5. Never have to go into an office.
6. Am actually using my MBA in Finance.
7. Have never "chatted" on the Internet.
8. Still own my vinyl records.
9. Donated money to several charities, received nice tax break.
10. Miss my girlfriend.

I stare at number ten for a long time and wonder why I deem that a positive quality. Isn't that just a normal response to sorrow? I mean, do I miss Susie or do I miss the "idea" of Susie? I'll have to think about that. Either way, it seems positive.

The negative:

1. Didn't listen to my uncle when he told me about Starbucks stock.
2. Only scored in the 75th percentile on the GMAT.
3. Don't know how to change a tire.
4. Don't own a dog.
5. Made Susie hate me.
6. Never call my mother.
7. Have bad choice in friends.

8. Don't eat enough fiber.
9. Eat a lot of red meat.
10. Am always making stupid lists and charts.

Number ten of the negatives seems a lot more honest than number ten on the positives, so I switch them. It gives both lists a sense of balance, I think.

I review my twenty attributes while I drink a cup of coffee and munch on a corned beef sandwich. Everything seems fine. There's a distinct ying and yang. Maybe there's even feng shui.

"Looks like you've got some bad karma working."

I look up and see that a waitress is reading my list over my shoulder.

"This is personal," I say and turn my pad over.

"Do you ever meditate or anything?"

"No," I say.

"You should," she says. "More coffee?"

"No thank you," I say.

The waitress reaches down and flips my pad back over. "Hmm," she says, running her finger down the page.

"What?"

"I tanked the GMAT," she says and then takes my coffee cup and empty plate.

At home, I look up the word *karma* in the dictionary. I know what the word means, but I've never really known what it *meant*. I decide I don't want to believe in karma. It doesn't matter anyway. If I believe in it, then whatever I've done in the past has already helped me or hurt me. If I don't believe in it and it still exists, well, then I'm working with a higher power that I just can't quantify.

I call Dan again.

"Listen," Dan says. "My time is used up."

"I need help with something," I say.

"Buy, sell, trade," Dan says. "Does that help?"

"Do you believe in karma?"

"Good karma or bad karma?"

"Is there a difference?"

Dan is silent.

"You still there?" I ask.

"I'm thinking," Dan says and is silent again.

I turn on CNBC and watch the ticker. AOL is down to 102. Starbucks is up three points. Callard & Bowser, the company that makes Altoids, is up two points. Microsoft is even...

"Okay," Dan says. "I'm done."

"What's your answer?"

"For you, yes, I believe in karma," Dan says. "For me it's a crap shoot."

"Where's this new job you've got?" I ask.

"Kinko's," Dan says. "Managing the night shift."

"Oh," I say. Dan is still not using his MBA. "You watching the ticker?"

"No," Dan says. "*Jerry Springer.*"

"So," I start to say, but Dan interrupts me.

"The answer is bad karma," Dan says.

"Any way to fix that?"

"Gotta give of yourself, my man," Dan says. "Maybe walk the earth like that dude from *Kung-Fu.* Helping people and shit."

"That seems a little too interactive," I say.

"Suit yourself," Dan says. "Maybe you can make pie graphs for people. You've always been pretty good at that."

"Susie didn't happen to call you, did she?"

"I'm gonna let you go now," Dan says and hangs up.

I sit at my desk and make a flow chart that clearly delineates how many good things I have done in my life and the positive events that directly followed them. I use colored pencils to illustrate the difference between my personal and financial success stories.

My companion chart shows any perceived negative actions and their subsequent results.

Susie calls just as I'm pinning the two charts to my cork board.

"I just wanted to see if you're all right," she says.

"I'm fine," I say. "Perfect."

"I know how you obsess," Susie says, "so don't think it's an appearance thing."

"I wouldn't," I say.

"How was the market today?"

"Down," I say.

"Look," Susie says after a while. "You and I just have different values. I mean, love is more than just sex and going to the movies and Thanksgiving with the family. There has to be some idea of hope."

"For what?"

"Growth. Change. Anything really," she says.

"And I don't have that?"

"Not right now," she says.

"Have you been talking to Dan?"

"He's a good friend to you," she says. "He told me you've been really upset."

"I'm fine." I pull my positive and negative flow charts off the cork board and crumple them into little balls.

"Do something constructive for a week or two," Susie says, "and then maybe we'll have lunch or something. Sort out whatever needs sorting out."

"Like getting back together?"

"Whatever," Susie says, and then: "I'd better let you go now."

"Why?" I say, but she's already gone.

I start simply. I write down on a 3 x 5 card the name of a stock I think is going to blow up in the next week, along with its NYSE or NASDAQ abbreviation, some quick background information on the company, and a suggestion of how much to invest. I then stick the card into an envelope along with a self-addressed stamped post-card with the number of a PO Box I've rented, and leave it where someone will find it. I leave these instructions inside:

Dear Person,

Enclosed please find an excellent investment tip. I have person-ally investigated this company and believe that you will see an awful lot of activity with its stock in the coming days. Please understand that this is a calculated gamble, but one that should pay off very well. If you choose to invest in this stock, please drop me a note using the enclosed postcard. Good luck!

My intention is to garner enough praise from this act of charity that I will be able to present Susie with a wide cross section of postcards that say what a kind and giving soul I am.

I leave my first envelope on an empty table at the California Pizza Kitchen on San Vicente. I sit by myself, right next to the table, and watch people being seated, waiting for the person who will get my gift.

He is tall with red hair and freckles and is wearing khaki pants with a blue shirt and blue tie and a rather prominent Kinko's name tag. His name is Rusty. I think it must be a nickname. Here is someone who needs my help.

Rusty flips through the menu and finally orders a small B.L.T. pizza and a diet 7-UP. He then stares out the window for a good ten minutes, never noticing the white envelope with some truly sound investment advice propped against the salt shaker.

"Can I borrow your salt?" I ask.

Rusty looks at me blankly.

"Your salt," I say, pointing in its direction. "Are you using it?"

Rusty shakes his head, like he's trying to loosen the moss, and then grabs the shaker and hands it to me. "Sorry," he says, almost sheepishly, "I was just zoning out."

"No problem," I say. "Smell of dittos always gave me a weird buzz when I was a kid, too."

Rusty gives me a look that says, "Fuck off, Mr. Tag Heuer Watch and Gucci Loafers," so I just get busy with my cold food and watch him out of the corner of my eye. He finally notices the envelope, toys with it for a couple of minutes, then shoves it into his breast pocket, checks around the room to see if anyone has noticed, eats his B.L.T. pizza, and leaves.

I call Dan that night. Susie answers the phone.

"What are you doing there?" I ask.

"I brought over a list of things I wanted Dan to get from the apartment for me," she says.

"Why are you answering his phone?"

"He's brushing his teeth."

I'm standing in my kitchen running scenarios: They've been sleeping together for years. She just needed someone to talk to. He's been sleeping with my girlfriend and claiming to be my best friend, all the while scheming to get rid of me. She's used me for investment purposes...

"Are you still there?" Susie asks.

"Yes," I say.

"Whatever you're doing," Susie says, "just stop right now, all right?"

"Sure," I say.

"I came by to give him a list of things, that's all," Susie says. "We've never slept together, we've never plotted against you, we've never done anything you are currently obsessing over."

"Okay," I say. "But how do I know that?"

"It's *Dan*," Susie says. "Give me some credit."

I don't say anything because I'm really thinking about this one.

"Listen," Susie says, "Dan is done brushing his teeth. Do you want to talk to him or do you just want to hang up and call back in five minutes when I'm gone?"

"You could come get your stuff yourself," I say. "I won't bite."

"I really don't want to sit around and cry with you," Susie says, but she sounds like she already is.

"I understand that," I say. "I've started doing some constructive things, you know, like you said."

"That's good," she says.

"I want you to know that I miss you," I say.

Nothing.

"And that I've made a few lists and graphs and things," I say, "and they all seem to show that we're just going through a downward trend. But, see, it's just a trend, and I'm doing some real positive things in the market to help massage the trend back into more of an upward slope."

Nothing.

"So, yes, it looks real good," I say. "Another rebound time for California-based products."

"I have to go," Susie says, and before I can say anything Dan is on the phone telling me that some crazy shit happened to a day-shift employee at his Kinko's.

"The kicker," Dan says, "is the kid called his dad, borrowed one hundred dollars and turned it into five hundred! Can you believe that?" Dan is speaking with a zest that's been missing since our first year in the MBA program at USC. "Made me want to put on a suit and tie again!"

"That's great," I say.

"No," Dan says, suddenly himself again, "it's sick. I went forty grand in debt so that I could pull that kinda shit off everyday, and this kid just walks into it."

"I'm gonna let you go now," I say.

After a week, I have nine postcards in my PO Box. I take them home and lay them out on my kitchen table and read each one carefully. They seem to follow a certain pattern, depending on the success of the stock and the amount invested. I've marked each postcard with a number that corresponds to a chart I'm keeping that clearly outlines where I've left envelopes.

Here is a sampling of my returns:

Dear Asshole,

You're a fucking sick bastard.

(I check and note that this envelope was left in the men's room of my gym.)

Dear Friend,

Thank you for the tip. Luckily, I've turned my life to Jesus Christ and no longer need material riches. However, I forwarded your message to my sister who invested $200 in Callard & Bowser and made a handsome return. May God's love shine upon you!

(Left at a bus stop on the corner of Wilshire and 26th Street)

To Whom It May Concern,

I found your envelope and thought it was some kind of practical joke, but then I watched how the stock performed over two days and found that your prediction was correct. Thanks so much...

(Left taped inside an elevator at 1920 Century Park East, Century City)

And so on. According to my records, I left thirty-six envelopes in various places over the past seven days, with a net return of nine responses. I deem this result well within my projected turnout.

Rusty didn't send me a postcard, but I feel like I don't really need one anyway.

For the second week, I decide to place an additional forty bits of financial advice around the city, including some areas that are more financially depressed than my general service area.

Dan calls me early Friday morning during week two of my experiment/plan to impress Susie and asks if I'll meet him for corn dogs on the Santa Monica Pier. I agree.

We walk along the pier eating our dogs and I can tell something is terribly wrong with Dan. For one thing, he's wearing a shirt that looks ironed. Of course, there's also the obvious fact that he called me and asked if I'd meet him for corn dogs on the Santa Monica Pier.

"Let me ask you something," Dan says. "How do you feel about the word *love*?"

"I think it's a good word," I say.

Dan takes a bite out of his corn dog and chews it slowly, like he's chewing my response. There's a dollop of mustard on his chin.

"Something wrong, Dan?"

"I've just been thinking about life lately," Dan says. "You know, your mind can wander when all you do is make photocopies all night."

"What does that have to do with love?"

"Well," Dan says, "I think I love your girlfriend and that's really fucking with my life right now. Can't eat, can't sleep, have trouble crapping, the whole nine. I feel like I'm walking around in a Neil Young song."

Dan has this queer smile on his face. I don't want to hit him; I don't even want to stomp away and make a scene. I mostly just want to hug him.

"That's a problem all right," I say eventually.

Dan just nods his head.

"Does she know this?" I feel like I'm talking about someone else's life, someone else's girlfriend, ex-girlfriend, whatever.

"Yeah," Dan says. "She feels the same way, I think."

"Oh."

We walk down toward the end of the pier, past the terrible Mexican restaurant that hangs over the ocean, and stop to watch an old Japanese man fish. He casts his line out and then mutters something under his breath. He repeats this same exact act five times in a row while Dan and I watch him.

"Are you mad?" Dan asks.

"I'm rather cross," I say.

It would be nice if I didn't think Susie defined me. It would be nice if I believed my own press: That I know how to read any market. That I know the personality of markets. That I know how to kiss and snuggle a market, make it feel comfortable in my hands, and then exploit it until it runs higher and higher and higher. It would be nice if I didn't really love Susie, which I think I do.

"I can see how you might feel that way," Dan says.

It's all gone, I think.

"I hope you two become very happy," I say. "Have loads of children and have a really nice CD collection and nonstick pans."

The Japanese man shrieks loudly and both Dan and I turn to watch him reel in some kind of very large fish.

"I wonder if his ambition in life is to catch fish," I say.

"Naw," Dan says. "His ambition is to eat the damn thing."

I go to the bank and withdraw $1000 in small bills. I go to Staples and buy twenty envelopes and twenty postcards. I go home and stuff envelopes with money. One person is going to get $200. Someone is going to get $10. Someone is going to get $31. You get the idea.

I call Susie's parents and ask if I may have their daughter's hand in marriage.

"I thought you two were broken up," Susie's mother says. Her dad is also on the line.

"No," I say. "We're just taking a break."

"The impression I got," Susie's dad says, "is that this was pretty final."

"You're mistaken," I say.

Nothing.

"In fact," I say, "as you well know, Mr. Klinger, with the success of the investments I've made for you, we are merely experiencing a slight drop-off in production right now. I believe that with a steady influx of capital, this relationship will prosper far into the future."

"Son," Susie's dad says, "I think you need help."

I stay up all night watching CNBC and planning where I will leave the money. I think about calling Susie and telling her that even if she loves Dan, and even if Dan loves her, I'm still doing something constructive. I think about calling her and telling her that even when we're not together, I still exist. I still have feelings and still have fears and ambitions and karma—this fucking issue of karma—I still have that. You know, I think about telling her, I still fucking *exist*.

But what's the point?

The point is that somewhere deep inside all of my charts and graphs and lists I think there is still faith and hope. Not that I know how to apply those rather oblique concepts to my life, but I think if I could just get to them, something good would happen. There's no use lying about it now—not while I'm mapping out where I'm going to leave small bundles of money.

I'm losing my freaking mind. It feels pretty good.

It's been nineteen days since I started leaving money for people. I have liquidated an eighteen-month CD (causing me to sacrifice a sizeable penalty) to finance this project. The Market has dropped 325 points over the past few days, which isn't exactly Black Tuesday because of the overall strength of the economy, but I'm aware that I should be dumping some stocks. AOL is down to 92. Bill Gates just sold off a million shares of Microsoft stock. Alan Greenspan, Chairman of the Federal Reserve Board, keeps appearing on the news. We've got troops massing on three different fronts to fight various and sundry UN-sanctioned wars.

I'm in my car sitting in front of Mail Boxes Etc. waiting for the mail to come. I haven't shaved in over a week because I keep breaking into hives, which is fine. I'm not trying to impress anyone.

Last night, Dan called to ask if he could stop by and get the rest of Susie's stuff.

"Tonight's not good for me," I said.

"What about tomorrow?"

"No," I said. "Tomorrow looks pretty bad."

"When does it look good?"

"Next Thursday," I said. "Maybe Friday. Call me."

Dan didn't respond so I just sat there and listened to him

breathe until he finally cleared his throat and started back up. "I'd appreciate it if you'd stop calling here all the time," Dan said. "You're scaring both of us."

"I don't know what you're talking about," I said.

"It's getting to the point where we might have to call the police," Dan said.

I hung up the phone, yanked the cord from the wall, went to the drawer next to the sink where I keep the tools, found my ball peen hammer, and smashed the phone to bits.

How do things end up this way? I ask myself. One minute Susie and I were taking walks along the Third Street Promenade, working out the names of our unborn children, holding hands, and kissing, and the next she thinks I may need to be incarcerated.

I go inside Mail Boxes Etc., nod at the clerk like I do everyday, and retrieve my booty.

Five samples from today's correspondence:

1. *I bought some dope stereo equipment with your $500. I ride the same bus every day, so just leave more money whenever you want.*
2. *I'm a single woman, with nice hips and a round ass. Are you single? Call me at 509-1998.*
3. *You're an angel sent from Jesus.*
4. *I saw you leave this. I know where you live. Bring another $1000 tomorrow or I'll kill you and your husband.*
5. *This is the kindest gesture a person has ever made. Oprah should do a whole episode about you!*

When I get home, Susie is standing in the kitchen, packing silverware.

"I let myself in," she says.

"That's fine," I say. "It's as much yours as it is mine." She's staring at my satchel overflowing with postcards. "I would have packed all of this up for you. All you had to do was ask."

On the kitchen table is a stack of twenties and several hundred envelopes that need to go out.

"I didn't want to bother you," Susie says.

"I've been busy," I say, "so maybe this is better."

The phone is scattered in pieces across the kitchen floor.

"What's going on here?" Susie says.

"I've been trying to do something constructive," I say. "I think I'm almost done. Are you ready for that lunch you promised?"

Susie sets the silverware down and picks up her car keys. "Look," she says. "I got most of what I wanted. You can keep the silverware."

"How are you and Dan doing?"

"Do you really want to know?"

"No," I say. "I see that you want to go, so that's fine. No time to discuss things."

Susie's hair is longer than I remember it, and her makeup seems softer.

"You look nice," I say. "Like when we first started dating."

"That was a long time ago," Susie says.

We are both just standing in the kitchen, and I start to become aware that Susie looks out of place. She looks like a Barbie doll in a cage of lions.

"I've been helping people," I say.

"I see that," Susie says, motioning to the wall where my top fifty postcards are taped up.

"Do you want to get something to eat with me?" I ask. "I could hop into the shower and we could go walk down Third Street."

"No," Susie says, "but thanks."

She picks up a garbage bag at her feet and makes her way to the door.

"Well," I say.

"I think you need to get some help," Susie says.

"Okay," I say.

"Whatever this is," Susie says, "it's not healthy."

"I'll keep that in mind," I say. I try to lean in toward Susie to kiss her on the cheek, just to let her know that I still care, but she pulls back quickly.

"Get help," she says and is gone.

The Market falls another 200 points, then rebounds 175, then drops and drops and drops. It doesn't matter. I'm all about being liquid. I sell my computers, my 5-Series BMW, anything worth selling.

Susie took all of her investment information with her that night she came by, plus her parents'. I've called to let her know that she needs to sell what she has. "Go liquid," I say into her answering machine. "The Market is all about growth and change," I say, "just like you always wanted."

"I know you love me," I say. "I know you've done this because you love me. I'd never have started divesting my money without you," I say. "I'm almost done. I'm almost completely out of everything," I say, "and I have documented proof that shows I'm making progress."

You can come home now.

THE LIVING END

In the summer of 1973, my father moved us from Reno to Yucca Valley; my brother came home from Vietnam; and Sarah Collins, the Indian girl with the Irish name, was kidnapped from in front of my house by two men in a cherry red El Camino.

I was thirteen that summer, and for many years since, I have thought about how I could have changed things had I only seen them a little more clearly, paid more attention to the small details, or even stepped onto my front porch a few minutes sooner. What I remember most about Sarah Collins is her face pressed up against the back window of the El Camino as it sped down our street. A big hand reached over her forehead and tried to pry her from the glass. On the middle finger was a silver ring that caught a ray of sunlight. I squinted from the glare and the car was gone.

We'd moved to Yucca Valley after my father was offered a job managing an Indian bingo parlor there. It was no secret that someday gambling was going to be legalized on Indian land in California, and already bingo parlors scattered between Upland and Indio were beginning to turn big profits. The Chuyalla Indians opened one off Interstate 10 just outside of Palm Springs and promised my father a percentage of the future take.

"This is a great opportunity for all of us," he said at the time. "The schools are better, we can have a big house, and I can make some real money." What he didn't know was that it would be seventeen years before the Indians would be allowed to put in blackjack tables and slot machines, that the fortunes would finally be made not by the pit bosses and concession managers, but by the Indian families who turned their plots of reservation land into gold mines. He also didn't know that he would die of leukemia before any of this happened.

My brother returned home from Vietnam the week before Sarah Collins was kidnapped. It was early July, a few days after the Fourth, and I rode with my mom out to the base at Twentynine Palms to meet him. Kenny was nine years older than me and had been in the Marines for four years. In the beginning, he sent letters every other day from boot camp, and then from jungle villages with names I couldn't pronounce. After his second year, though, the letters had come less and less often, making us worry until, after a while, even Mom got used to his silences.

I sat in the front seat of my mother's idling Volkswagen, the desert air heavy and dense in the midafternoon sun, and found myself wondering what I would say to this brother whom I really knew nothing about anymore.

"There he is," my mother said, and jumped out of the car. In the distance, Kenny emerged through the front gate of the base, a knapsack slung over his shoulder. He looked gaunt, his skin hanging like a wet rag over his face. His uniform was plastered to him by sweat, and his eyes were hidden behind a pair of aviator glasses. When my mother rushed up to him, he dropped the knapsack and threw his arms around her.

I got out of the car and waited by the front bumper. My mom held Kenny's hand while they walked, swinging it back and forth. In all her life, I don't think there was a single moment when she looked more beautiful.

When they reached the car, Kenny stood up straight and gave me a salute. My mom giggled like a teenager. "Look at you," he said. "Practically turned into a man while I was gone." He tousled my hair and I squirmed away from him.

"Cut it out," I said. "I hate that."

"Do I at least get a hug?" Kenny pulled down his glasses and smiled at me. His eyes were bloodshot and all pupils. "Or isn't that the cool thing anymore?"

I put my arms around his waist and hugged him. His body was lean and hard and I could feel his ribs and spine through his shirt, and it occurred to me that I couldn't remember ever hugging him before, not even when he left.

"It's good to see you Teddy," he said. "It is so good to finally see you again."

On the ride back home, Kenny told us about how wet and hot Vietnam was, and how the mosquitoes there would tug at your skin until it broke open in raised welts. He leaned into the back seat and pushed up his sleeve to show me the scars. Thin black lines crisscrossed his forearm, disappearing beneath the hair that crawled just above his elbow.

"Tell your brother everything he's missed," Mom said. "Tell him everything on your list, Teddy."

Before Kenny left, he told me to keep track of things, to keep a running tally of life so that when he came home, he could fall back into step. He told me to keep a scrapbook and to draw pictures and to memorize entire baseball games. I'd done those things for a few months, and then I stopped and lived my life, because after a time that's all I could be expected to do.

So I told him about the A's winning the World Series and about Jennifer Sedgwick kissing me during a school play and about what it was like packing the house up, but Kenny wasn't really listening. He rubbed his left hand over his forearm, sometimes scratching at the scars there. Mom patted his hand gently.

"Sorry," Kenny said to Mom. "It's a habit. What else, Teddy? There must be more."

I didn't say anything for a moment. We were still only a few miles from the base, and the cars on either side of us all held soldiers coming home. A couple of times Kenny gave mock salutes to guys I assumed he knew. Finally, as we merged onto the interstate, I said, "How many people did you kill?"

Sarah Collins and her family lived across the street from us in a house exactly like ours. And like the one next to us. And the one behind us. Sarah's father, a big Chuyalla Indian named Harley Collins, worked with my dad at the bingo parlor as the Chief of Security. He had a boxer's face, nose flattened across his cheeks and hooded eyes heavy with scar tissue. Sarah's mother had emphysema. She would sit outside some nights and cough and cough until I wondered if she might tear out her throat.

On July 14, a Thursday, Sarah Collins sat on the sidewalk drawing chalk lines on the asphalt for hopscotch. She was eight years old, with a pixie haircut, a blue striped shirt, red dolphin shorts, and sandals—brown buckled sandals. I was shooting baskets with my brother in our driveway. I was Elvin Hayes hitting perfect fallaway jumpers; he was Lew Alcindor sky-hooking over my head. Kenny would drive on me, his body all sinew and scars beneath a thin veil of sweat, drop a step, then arc the ball into the basket. Once, when the ball got away from us and rolled into the street, Sarah picked it up, bounced it twice using both hands, and heaved it back to me. She was just a little girl.

Kenny beat me, making his shots with intensity, muscling me during nervous collisions. He had a look about him that said, *Things are not right with me; better just let me pass.* And I did, until point number twenty-one fell through the hoop and I sat down on the grass to catch my breath.

Sarah tossed a rock across a set of stacked squares she had drawn on the street, then hopped, one foot tucked behind her thigh, down a long row and picked up the rock again. It was nearly 110 degrees that day, and watery mirages hung just above the pavement. Sarah hopped again and then tripped, skinning her knee on the hot asphalt. She got up quickly and looked my way, her face tense, tears already beginning to roll down her cheeks.

"Are you hurt?" I asked.

Sarah didn't say anything, just shook her head slowly. I walked over to where she was standing and took a look at her knee. It was bleeding now, a thin trickle running down to her sandaled foot.

"If I go inside and get you a Popsicle," I asked, "will you stop crying?"

Sarah nodded yes.

I walked back across the street to my house and was opening the front door when Sarah called out to me.

"My favorite flavor is orange!" she shouted from the middle of the street. A red El Camino pulled onto our block then. Sarah stepped onto the curb, and I went inside.

What happened next I don't know exactly. Maybe they offered her a piece of candy, or asked if her mommy was home; or maybe they just slowed to a crawl, and the guy with the silver ring jumped out, grabbed her by the hair, and tossed her in.

When I came back out with two orange Creamsicles, still wrapped, in my hands, the El Camino was screeching down the street. And there was Sarah Collins in the rear window. And there was that flash of sunlight off that silver ring. And there—standing in the side yard—was Kenny, a joint pressed between his lips, his face drawn and slack.

The police questioned me for more than two hours hoping for a detail that might help them find Sarah Collins. They showed me mug shots, but I hadn't seen a face. They also questioned Kenny. He told them that he'd walked outside the same moment I had, and that all he'd seen was the car, nothing else. I told them I hadn't even known Kenny was there.

Afterward, Kenny and I sat in the living room and stared out to the street, where Harley Collins, still in his Tribal Police uniform, was holding his screaming wife, Nora. She was screaming up at the sky, rocking slowly back and forth, begging God, or whomever she prayed to, to bring her daughter back. Kenny was stoned, his eyes half open. Our parents were outside talking with the neighbors. As we sat in the half-light of dusk, I found myself staring at my brother.

"Don't look at me," he said.

I wasn't, exactly. I was staring at his arms. There were fresh pinpoint scars just above his wrists. "Why didn't you tell them what you saw?" I said.

"I didn't see a fucking thing," he said, then pushed me down into the couch, his face inches from mine. His breath, stale from marijuana, was all over me. He put a knee into my sternum, forcing all the air from my lungs. "Not a fucking thing, you hear?"

The front door opened and Kenny rolled off of me. Mom and Dad came in and found me on the couch gasping for breath.

"It's all right, Teddy," Dad said, thinking I was crying. "There was nothing you could have done."

I looked up and saw Kenny walking out the door.

A police car rolled up and down our street on the hour every hour, but it was useless. The kidnappers had come and gone, and it stood to reason they weren't hiding in the bushes with Sarah. A group of about thirty Indian men gathered out in front of the Collins's house with flashlights. My dad said they all worked at the parlor. "The Indians," he said, "take care of their own."

My father went outside and talked with them, though he wasn't real friendly with most of the workers. The Indians didn't like having people from outside the tribe working in the parlor, especially someone who was hoping to cash in on their future. But Harley and my dad were friends, and Dad wanted to help with the search.

My mother was standing on the front porch smoking a cigarette. I came out and sat down on one of the steps.

"Your father is going out to hunt for Sarah," she said, smoke twisting out of her nose. It was close to ten o'clock at night, but the thermometer still hovered near a hundred degrees. "What do you think about that?"

"Seems like a waste of time," I said.

My mother sat down next to me and put her arm over my shoulder. It was hot and sweaty. "Don't know what good these men can do," she said, "except get that poor girl killed if they stumble on her."

Two big flatbed trucks pulled up and everyone piled in. My father gave us a little wave as they departed.

"Let's move back to Reno," I said. "I don't like it here."

My mother pulled me to her and kissed me on the forehead. "Things will get better," she said. "You'll start school in a couple of months, and all of this will seem like ancient history."

So, on a smoldering night in the low desert, as the wind picked up and the sand foxes howled their low whines, I lay sleepless on the bottom bunk of the bed I shared with Kenny. He was writhing above me, shouting to some battalion that had walked across his dreams. Sarah Collins was gone, and I'd never even known her. In the final moments, had she spotted Kenny standing there, watching her being abducted? Had she cried out to him for help?

For two weeks, Sarah Collins was on the front page of the *Riverside Press-Enterprise* and the *Palm Springs Desert Sun*. Then she was on page three. After a month, she was moved to the local news section. By September, Sarah Collins was gone.

At night Harley Collins sat out on his front porch with a flashlight, the beam scanning every bush, stopping on anything that moved in its sweeping arc. Nora Collins rarely set foot outside the house; but when she did, she would stare right through you, her face bloodless and long.

As the summer drifted away, Kenny began to disappear for hours at a time, reappearing shirtless and sunburned. Once, late at night, I saw him climb naked out our bedroom window and slip into the street. Crouching, he grabbed a handful of rocks and rubbed them across his body until his stomach and arms were covered in red marks. I closed our window and latched it firmly, then locked our bedroom door. When I awoke the next morning, I found him asleep on the couch under an old afghan.

Since the day Sarah was kidnapped, I'd tried to take note of the smallest details in Kenny's behavior. I didn't exactly blame him, but I was afraid of him. I knew that his threat to me was real enough and that there were things about Kenny I would never understand.

One day, underneath his mattress, I found two long needles, their tips brown and sharp, and a picture of Sarah clipped from the newspaper. In the article, both Sarah's name and mine were underlined with thin blue pen, but Kenny's was not. There was also a small gun dug into his mattress.

My father got Kenny a job parking cars at the bingo parlor, but Kenny was asked to quit after one hundred dollars came up missing during his shift twice in the same week. He blamed the Indians. "They have it in for me, Dad," he said as we sat at the table eating dinner. My dad just nodded and continued to read the paper. "It's all because of that dumb little girl. They think because I look a little different I had something to do with it." He had a patchy beard now, and his hair, uncut since he'd come home, was tied into a greasy ponytail.

"Did you?" I said.

My mother told me to stop acting like a child, then just shook her head back and forth. "That's just ludicrous," she said.

"Tell Dad that," Kenny said.

"No, it's ludicrous that you are blaming Sarah," my mom said. "Really, Kenny, have some compassion."

Kenny glared at her. He turned his head and gave me an uneven smile. "You wanna shoot some hoops, Teddy?" he asked.

We hadn't played basketball since that day: July 14, 1973. A Thursday.

"That's a good idea," my dad said suddenly. "Why don't you two go outside? I want to talk to your mother."

The sun had just set behind the San Jacinto Mountains, and already Harley was out on his porch with his flashlight. I was sitting across the street from him, lacing up my shoes, when the light trained on my face. Kenny was still inside changing clothes. Harley let the light search my entire body—from my face down to my throat, across my chest and arms, and finally over my legs and feet. I stood up and walked to the edge of our grass.

"How are you, Mr. Collins?" I called to him.

He'd followed me with the light all the way to where I stood. He didn't answer me for a long time.

"I'm at the dead end of life," he said finally. "Tell me, was she happy before they came?"

"Yes, sir, she was," I lied. I didn't want to tell him about her knee being split open, about the blood staining her little sandal. I didn't want to tell this man, who drove a van with a scenic outlay of the Old West painted on one side, that I thought his little girl was buried somewhere beneath the scorching desert floor.

Harley clicked his flashlight off, and I heard him cough. "One day your life just melts away," he said, "and terror moves in."

Behind me, I heard Kenny walking down the driveway bouncing the basketball. "I'm sorry," I said. "I wish I could remember more about the car, or about the men, or about anything. It just happened so fast…."

Harley put his hand up to stop me. "There is a story in our tribe," he said. "We believe all the dead children visit us at night. They come into our dreams and we are not afraid, because death is a life-giver and a life-taker, a beginning and an end. They give us great joy and also terrible nightmares, but when we wake they are still a part of us, if only for that one moment when we can remember them. Still in our skin and teeth and hair. They are the cause of all tears and laughter." Harley stood up and set his flashlight down on his seat. "As in life. And you know something? I'd give anything for her to be here, right now, or to simply know where she is. Dead or alive."

Kenny stood beside me now, his hand pressed between my shoulders, and made a noise under his breath as Harley slipped quietly inside his house. "Crazy fucking Indian," Kenny said.

I wanted to grab my brother by the throat and twist the hate out of him, squeeze whatever was lurking just below his skin to the surface, force him to the ground and let the bugs take him apart piece by piece. Our eyes met, like they had that July day, and Kenny held my gaze until I shivered.

We played Twenty-One again that night, Kenny moving like a hunted animal. He would lean against me when I had the ball, his body low to the ground as though he might pounce. Whenever he went up for a jump shot, he'd let out a little hiss from his nose. Before the final point, Kenny pulled off his shirt: raised welts covered his back and chest. There were new scratches and deep gashes in his forearms, as if he'd been clawed.

Kenny stood at the top of the key, his chest heaving for air, his skin flushed with abrasions. With a swivel step he crossed his dribble over and came into the lane. I stepped in front of him, hoping he would stop and pull up a jumper so that I could go inside, wash his sweat off my body, and try to avoid him. Instead, he lowered his shoulder and plowed into me, sending me skidding across the blacktop. Then, with a flick of his wrist, Kenny banked a shot into the basket to defeat me.

The ball rolled down the driveway, bumped over the hard asphalt where Sarah Collins skinned her knee, and came to rest against the sidewalk in front of the Collins's home. Kenny stood above me, his breath slowing. He frowned at me lying there on the ground, and shook his head lightly. "Good game, Teddy," he said and walked into the house.

Later that night, as I sat on the front porch listening to a Dodgers game over my red transistor radio, my dad came out and sat down next to me. He was already fifty years old and gray hair flecked the stubble that grew on his chin. We sat together for a long while, not speaking, just listening to Vin Scully call balls and strikes. In Reno, before Kenny went away, the three of us had often gone to see the local minor league team play. My father liked to watch the players—some just old enough to vote—sign autographs and live out their country-boy dreams. Once, when the Oakland A's played an exhibition against the Seattle Pilots there, Dad pulled some strings at the casino and we got to meet a few of the players. Billy North, Joe Rudi, and Vida Blue all signed a ball for me, while Dad cornered a young Reggie Jackson and told him he would be better than Roberto Clemente. Kenny had Catfish Hunter sign nearly every article of clothing he had on.

"Your mom and I thought a camping trip might be good for all of us," my dad said now. "Maybe go up to Julian or Joshua Tree. What do you say?"

"Sounds okay," I said.

Dad was staring down at his feet. He had gathered a pile of pebbles and was tapping them back and forth. "Then, after we get back, we'll see if we can't get Kenny some help."

I'd been afraid my parents hadn't noticed anything, and was relieved to find out that I was wrong.

"Maybe some time away," Dad said. "You know, to get his head straightened out."

Vin started up again and my dad stopped talking. If I'd known then that in ten years I'd be watching him slowly wither away until I wished that he would die, and then be standing at his grave watching dirt fall over his casket, I might have told him right then and there that I loved him; that children are never done growing, and that his elder boy might be okay one day.

Long after the game had ended, Dad and I sat there and listened to an AM station broadcasting out of Mexico. The desert air was filled with the smell of the coming fall, the wind dense with pollen. While my father and I listened to the distant cackle of the radio, I saw Harley Collins pull back his blinds and peek out at us. My dad gave him a brusque wave, and Harley clicked off the lights in his living room.

"Do you think they'll ever find Sarah?" I asked.

My dad tilted his head back toward the stars and rubbed his eyes. "No," he said. "I really don't."

That following weekend—the weekend before I'd start high school—we packed up the truck and headed east on Highway 62 to Joshua Tree National Monument. There we pitched our two tents in a valley surrounded by low brush and six-foot Joshua trees. After we unpacked, my mother and I went looking for kindling while Kenny and my dad dug a fire pit.

The sun was beginning to set and a cool mountain breeze was blowing from the north as my mother and I climbed a ridge just above the valley floor. She still looked young then, with her sandy blond hair tied back behind her. She *was* young, really—only forty, having married my dad when she was nineteen.

In the distance, I could see my brother and father shoveling dirt and sand. My mother stopped to watch, too. "Your brother looks just like your father from here," she said, stuffing a handful of twigs into my backpack. "Not the hair, of course, but his body and the way he walks." It was true: they both had a loose, athletic shuffle and rounded shoulders that made them look like they were hunched over. "But you," she continued, "you've got the good looks from the other side of the family." She smiled and brushed the bangs from my eyes. I walked on up the path, but my mom stood there for a time with her hands on her hips, biting her bottom lip, watching my brother and father.

For dinner we roasted hot dogs over the fire and drank strawberry Shasta. The moon was only a sliver that night and the sky glittered with a million silver bulbs while Dad and Kenny told ghost stories until Mom got frightened and made them stop, only to beg them to continue again. And in the quiet between stories, I looked across the licking flames of our campfire and saw Kenny smiling, and next to him my mother and father holding hands and giggling. For an instant, I thought maybe things were going to turn out all right; that our lives, while fractured, weren't all that different from anyone else's.

We spent the rest of the evening telling stories and eating s'mores, talking about everything except Sarah Collins and Kenny. As the fire cooled, my parents came to Kenny and me and kissed us gently on our heads and told us goodnight. It was a moment of simple perfection that has been forever frozen into my mind.

I'd been asleep for hours, my dreams troubled by visions of that cherry red El Camino, when I was awakened by the roar of the wind as it slapped at our tent, the nylon door rippling against the frame. I turned over and saw that Kenny's sleeping bag was empty and that his clothes were folded neatly beside his pillow, his shoes and socks placed beside the door.

I got up and unzipped the flap and found Kenny sitting beside the fire pit, his naked back covered in dark, burnt slashes that bled in thin trails. I watched him reach into the dead fire again and again, pull out still-hot cinders, and press them into his back until his skin sizzled. He made no noise as his flesh burned, only jerked his back inward, then repeated the process.

I was scared then, not only for Kenny, but for myself. Scared that he might hurl himself into the pit, might twist his body in mad circles until all that remained was ash, scared that he might take me with him. I let out a little squeak through my clenched teeth and Kenny turned and saw me there in the entrance to our tent. He rose up on his knees and crawled toward me, his chest a charred map of welts and deep, bleeding burns. I slid back into the tent and pulled my sleeping bag up over my body as Kenny edged in beside me, the tent filling with the acrid smell of his burning flesh and hair. He lay there naked and stared at me, his lips moving, his breath beating out of him in staccato bursts.

"It's good now, isn't it?" he said, his voice no more than a whisper. "It's good, right?"

I closed my eyes and tried to find a different place in my mind, a place far away from the tent and my smoldering brother, a place I might find Sarah. I flew over the Joshua trees, down an endless desert plain, across Whitewater River and through the open dunes. And I found her, her skin bleached albino white by the sun, her perfect features washed out, her pixie haircut matted above the hollow of her face. She was dead, the little Indian girl who lived across the street from me, the little Indian girl whose father died every night, the little Indian girl whose father had a van painted with these very same Joshua trees, a bucking bronco, an impossible sunset. Harley Collins would never see his girl grow up, would never get to see her in her Sunday best, her prom dress, her first kiss, her last breath, because maybe I'd witnessed it all for him. For her. Maybe I'd witnessed the end of it all for the father of that sweet, innocent, little Indian girl.

As my brother mumbled and his charred body shook in our tent, I discovered an even scarier place, the place where that little girl's life had come full circle, and Death had stopped long enough to dance by the fire and take her pain away and leave me here, alone, with another dying child.

COMEBACK SPECIAL

My picture of Elvis is bleeding. It's from his 1968 NBC Comeback Special, so he's wearing that black leather outfit and he's still skinny and handsome. The bleeding started with just a trickle out of his right eye, no bigger than a tear, really.

The picture wasn't exactly mine. It belonged to Sharon, my ex, so I called her when it started happening.

"Your Elvis picture is bleeding," I said.

"We're not getting back together," Sharon said and hung up.

I'm not even an Elvis fan.

"We gotta go to Tennessee," my brother Jack said when he saw it. "Do you realize the kind of money this thing would get down there? He's like the freaking king of the state."

The day before Elvis started bleeding, I cleaned up the house, again, trying to make sense of how Sharon was able to cheat on me with my best friend *and* get all the good furniture. She was kind enough to let me keep my dog. My house was a lot easier to clean, though, with just an easy chair and a stack of magazines to negotiate around.

When I saw Elvis up there on the wall, I thought, Goddamn, she forgot something. My first instinct was just to chuck the thing. My second was to throw it on the floor and jump on it.

But then I got to looking at the picture, and I thought, Hell, it isn't offending me with its presence. It's not like Elvis left me. So I kept it up. I even sprayed some Endust on the imitation wood frame.

That night I sat up in bed and read every catalog I could find. I piled through *Victoria's Secret, Lands' End, J.Crew,* and even an old *Sears* catalogue from six Christmases ago. With a black marker, I circled all the things I thought Sharon might have liked for her birthday and Valentine's Day, even Mother's Day, though we don't have any kids. I also found a couple of things I thought she might have purchased for me for the same holidays, and a couple extra just for being the man she loved. Then, using the new Visa card that came for her in the mail that day, I ordered everything.

When I still couldn't fall asleep, I went out onto the front porch with my cocker spaniel, Chester, and listened to the cars racing down the interstate. The dog and I sat there for a long time and I thought that things weren't really so bad. I was still pretty young, still good looking, and still in love with my ex. So what? I rubbed Chester's belly and he made this soft humming noise out of his nose, and every now and then he'd lean up and lick my arm with slow, deliberate strokes.

"I hate the way you let that dog lick you," Sharon used to say. "He's probably just tenderizing you."

After a while, when I'd decided that the only thing worse than being with someone who didn't love you anymore was being by yourself, I headed off to bed and hoped that the next day things would start to get better.

"Way I see it," my brother Jack said, "this is some kind of sign."

"Maybe the Endust I rubbed on the frame made a chemical reaction," I said.

Jack shook his head. "No way," he said. "Elvis is bleeding *under* the glass. This is unexplained phenomena." We were both sitting on the floor of my living room staring at Elvis and drinking beer. Chester was asleep on the easy chair, snoring.

"What now?" I asked.

"Hell if I know," Jack said. "He hasn't been singing or anything, has he?" Jack got up off the floor and walked over to the wall where Elvis was and stared at the picture for a long time. "I guess just let the sucker bleed," Jack said. "I mean, it's not like he's going to die."

"Don't go telling anyone about this," I said. "Last thing in the world I need right now is Barbara Walters showing up with a camera crew."

"Barbara Walters wouldn't show up," Jack said, seriously, still staring at Elvis. "But you might get Geraldo Rivera or maybe that foxy Katie Couric." Then Jack started tapping his foot and singing "Hound Dog."

After Jack left, still humming Elvis tunes, I pulled the picture off the wall, carefully unscrewed the back of the frame and slipped the picture out. I turned it over in my hands, careful not to smudge any blood on my new jeans, and then slowly ran my palm over the surface of the photo, avoiding Elvis's right eye.

The texture was smooth and glossy, no visible bumps or cuts. I touched the bridge of Elvis's nose with my pinky. It was warm. It wasn't pulsing, and it certainly wasn't taking in air, but it did have a certain warmth to it. I'm no doctor, so I can't say if it was 98.6 degrees warm or 75 degrees warm, or what. I'm just saying it was warm enough to freak me out.

Elvis kept bleeding on his leather jumpsuit for three days. Then, on a Tuesday morning, I woke up to find Elvis wearing black shades and a karate outfit. There was blood coming from underneath the shades. He didn't look any more upset than he had in the 1968 Comeback Special photo that was in the frame when I went to sleep the night before.

I called Sharon again, because, frankly, this was starting to get to me, and my dog seemed bothered by the change as well. He was sitting under the picture growling.

"Don't hang up on me," I said when Sharon answered the phone.

"It's over," she said. "Just get that through your narrow little head."

"It's about your Elvis picture," I said.

"Look," Sharon said. "I'm not coming over there so you and I can rehash ancient history again. I love Cal now."

"It's still bleeding," I said.

"Grow up, Tom." Sharon hung up.

I waited a few seconds—for what I'm not sure—and then hung up, too. Chester was still sitting under the picture with his teeth bared and his ears flat against the side of his head.

I hadn't gotten too close to the picture since I felt how warm Elvis's nose was, but I figured spontaneous outfit changes did require some investigation. This time, though, I took a few precautions. I went into the kitchen and put on a pair of rubber gloves and an apron. And this time I found out not only was Elvis warm, but his blood tasted like blood.

Jack showed up at my house just after noon wearing a new shirt and tie with some fancy slacks. He seemed nervous. "Anybody been by here since yesterday?" he asked.

"No," I said. "But Elvis is changing."

"He hasn't stopped bleeding, has he?"

"No," I said. "But he decided to slip into something less flattering." It was true; Elvis didn't look quite as good in the karate outfit as he had in the leather.

"This is bad," Jack said when he saw the picture. "He's getting older. Don't you see? This picture is 1972, maybe a little later."

"What does it matter?"

Jack sat down in the easy chair and loosened up the tie he was wearing. "I told the television people he was wearing the leather outfit. Do you know how popular that Elvis era is?"

"Jack," I said.

"You know, this kind of opportunity comes but once in a lifetime."

"Jack."

"The buses should be here before one, two o'clock tops."

"I have to tell you," the woman in my living room said, "if my momma were alive today, she would just die." The woman was wearing a T-shirt with little teddy bears stitched onto the fabric.

She also wore a backpack with an enormous picture of the Starship Enterprise darting into space. "This is just the most special thing I have ever seen."

"Thank you," Jack said, because I wasn't much in the mood for talking. "We think we're just a little bit blessed for having you in our home."

I walked outside and stood on my front porch. It was three o'clock in the afternoon and there were at least 200 people in line to get into my living room. There was a guy with a pushcart selling laminated pictures of Elvis. Two kids with pinwheels were running shirtless across my front lawn. It had been like this for over two weeks.

"Isn't this great?" Jack said after he ushered the teddy bear/*Star Trek* woman outside. "How would you feel about getting a band?"

"I wouldn't," I said.

There were RVs parked bumper to bumper along the curb in front of my house and people were barbecuing hamburgers and drinking sodas. The Channel 13 *Action News* van blocked my driveway while they conducted exit interviews with the folks who'd seen Elvis.

"What about karaoke?"

My next-door neighbor, Irene, was charging five dollars for people to park on her driveway. The Red Cross set up a tent to treat all the people who'd been passing out.

"Has Sharon called today?" I asked.

"No," Jack said.

A priest and two nuns waved signs that said PRAY TO SAINTS, NOT PAGANS toward a tight mob of people.

"Someone could get hurt out here with all this traffic," I said. "Maybe we could set up a sand box or something for the kids."

"That's just what I'm trying to get at!" Jack said. "But something more interactive."

The crowd surrounding the priest and two nuns turned around when the priest pointed toward Jack and me and shook his sign.

Then *everyone* stopped and looked at us. The people in line, the man selling *churros*, the kids with the pinwheels, the cop writing a parking ticket, everyone.

When Sharon and I first started dating, she made me listen to a self-help tape that she said would improve the quality of my life. Every time we got into the car this booming voice would come out of the radio and say, "Perspective. Use it or lose it! Remember where you are going and why you created the mess you've gotten yourself into!"

I went inside, opened a can of Alpo for Chester, and watched reruns of old game shows while Jack ushered in the worshippers.

Elvis is fat and bleeding profusely from his eyes and ears. Jack tells me the outfit he's wearing is exactly what he wore in his last TV special, *Aloha from Hawaii*.

Here is what I've learned about Elvis since this began: He was born on January 8, 1935. He died on August 16, 1977. Here is what I have witnessed in person: Between 1968 and 1975, he gained an awful lot of weight, started crying tears of blood, and eventually moved into full-body stigmata. Now, in his current state of photographic unrest, he's pretending he's contracted the Ebola virus. All of this in my living room.

Meanwhile, my brother Jack has dyed his hair black, affected some kind of pseudo Southern accent, and started calling women "Darlin'." My dog Chester stopped eating for a couple of days, but the tourists kept giving him handfuls of Cracker Jacks and the crusts from their homemade sandwiches, so he has managed to pull through all right.

Sharon showed up yesterday. She waited until most of the people had left, after midnight, then walked into her old house wearing a scarf and a pair of black Ray-Bans, like she thought I wouldn't recognize her.

"That's not my picture," Sharon said. "I hate this Elvis. He was already shooting TVs and pissed off about Priscilla."

"I tried to tell you." A bus of Japanese tourists pulled up across the street and started unloading cameras and video recorders from their bags. "Jack," I said, "tell them we're closed. It's almost one in the morning for God's sake."

"They've come a long way for this," Jack said. He was wearing a red, white, and blue jumpsuit with collars the size of pizzas.

"I'm tired as hell," I said, "and I've gotta walk Chester." Jack shrugged and made his way over to the bus.

Sharon sat down in the easy chair and took off her disguise. "I appreciate all those gifts you sent me."

"Sorry about the bills," I said. "You kind of caught me at a bad time."

"Jack seems to be in his element," Sharon said. My brother was talking to the tourists out front, explaining to them that Elvis would still be here tomorrow.

"He's found his calling," I said.

"I don't want you to think the wrong thing about me coming over," Sharon said. "This is strictly about Elvis."

Jack walked back inside and went straight to the refrigerator for a beer. He came into the living room with his jumpsuit unbuttoned down to his belly button and one of my baseball caps on his head.

"You look good, Jack," Sharon said. "You should move to Vegas."

"These Japanese tourists don't understand the concept of time change," Jack said. "They get off the damn plane and it's noon in Taiwan, or wherever the hell they're from, and they think it's kosher to come into an American neighborhood at freaking midnight. No sense of decorum, you know?"

"You're all class," Sharon said, then stood up to look more closely at Elvis. "You making any money from this, Tom?"

"Enough to reseed the lawn. It's been trampled up pretty good."

"I want to go down more of merchandising road," Jack said. "But Tom's against it."

Sharon ran her finger around the edges of the picture frame.

"This is a crappy frame," she said. "With all these people coming through here, you could have at least spruced it up some."

"I don't think they much care," I said. "Most of them have fainted by the time they're close enough to actually study it."

"Cal wanted me to take it back," Sharon said.

"Cal is a son of a bitch," Jack announced. "First he steals my brother's wife and now he's going to take Elvis? I don't think so. I'll kick his teeth in if he even comes near the King. You tell him that, Sharon."

"Calm down, Jack," Sharon said. "I don't want the damn thing. It gives me the willies."

"I don't understand why this is happening," I said. "The only Elvis song I know by heart is 'Sweet Caroline.'"

"That's Neil Diamond," Sharon said and gave me a little pat on the head like she used to do when I was looking cute to her. "Anyway, I think you should have some professionals look at it. Who knows what kind of diseases you could be exposing people to."

"I was kind of hoping this might die down in the next week or two," I said.

It's a Thursday night, six weeks since this all started, and Jack and I are in New York sitting in the green room waiting for David Letterman to call my name. Elvis is packed away in an airtight, vacuum-sealed, double-insulated glass box. He's wearing a skintight, white, gold, red, purple, and pink jumpsuit that's covered in glitter. He's fatter now, by twenty pounds at least. There are three sweat-drenched towels around his neck, and he's leaning over into the audience. A young woman's arm can be seen wrapping around the King's neck. There is a thin trail of blood running from his left eye down toward his mouth. Most people who've seen the picture believe he is singing the chorus to "Suspicious Minds."

This is what I've learned: Elvis's middle name is Aron. On his birth certificate it is spelled "Aron"; on his death certificate it is spelled "Aaron." This misspelling is what most people point to as the reason they believe Elvis is alive.

For the first five years I was in school, Castle Rock Elementary had my name spelled Thom. All of my school pictures from first through fifth grade say my name is "Thom Leeds." I had trouble learning how to read because I'm dyslexic, so it took me a while to realize the error.

As far as I know, that is the only thing Elvis and I share.

"You think we might end up on one of those programs on *E!*?" Jack asks.

"Depends how quotable I am," I say. Jack can't stop fidgeting in his seat, and it's making me nervous. He keeps getting up and looking out into the hallway, like he is waiting for someone.

"You should have worn something a little flashier," Jack says. I have on a pair of tan Dockers and a new shirt from the Gap. "Harrison Ford would have put on an Armani suit for this."

"I'm not Harrison Ford," I say.

"Well," Jack says, "we're dealing with history here and you look like a bumpkin."

The "history" we were dealing with is all Jack's idea, truth be told. After Sharon came by, Jack got it in his head that maybe we ought to have some scientific tests done on the picture. "We might make it into a textbook or something," he said. Jack made a mistake then. He called Graceland. "They're sending a team of doctors and some forensic detectives."

"I don't know about this," I said, but Jack seemed to believe that it would add some legitimacy to our cause.

"This isn't a cause to me," I said.

"Look outside, Tom," Jack said. "See all those people? They came here because they believe in this thing. They probably think you're some kind of messiah just for having the damn thing in your living room."

"It's not even mine!"

I had to give Jack some credit, though, because he was right about one thing. As much as I hated the lines of tourists, all the buses and motor homes parked up and down the block, it felt pretty good to see people having so much faith in something. I've never been a religious man, or even much into rock and roll, but when I saw some of those purple-hairs walking up to my front door just hoping to get a glimpse of Elvis, I did feel a bit proud.

Two days after the call to Graceland, a white bus pulled up onto my driveway at 7:30 in the morning and fifteen guys in lab coats came rolling out like I shot the President. They had cell phones and Palm Pilots coming out of every pocket and these official-looking badges that said GRACELAND MEDICAL ADVISORY stuck to their lapels.

"Looks like they've done this sort of thing before," Jack said.

First thing they wanted to do was take a blood sample from Chester.

"It is common practice, Mr. Leeds," one of the doctors said. "We always match the DNA of any localized pets in a case like this."

"This isn't a case," I said, "and you're not touching my dog."

"Mr. Leeds, you asked us here," the doctor said. "We can just as easily pack up our tools and leave."

Jack grabbed my arm. "Hey now," he said. "Let's not get jumpy here. If we get some kind of official seal of approval from these guys, we're talking international promotional appeal. You're looking at breakfast cereals and trading cards."

"It just seems stupid," I said. "The poor dog is already wound up pretty tightly."

"He won't feel a thing, right, doctor?"

"Not really," said the doctor.

"All right," I said finally. "Just don't hurt him."

The doctors took blood from Chester, then Jack, and me before touching Elvis. "This is very odd," one of the doctors said after examining the picture. "You say that Mr. Presley has been changing outfits?"

"And poses," I said.

"As far as I can tell, and this is just a rudimentary evaluation, it appears that Mr. Presley is wearing the same undergarments that he fashioned for the original performance photo; which is to say none."

I didn't say anything because, well, I didn't really have a response for that. But two other doctors immediately began examining the photo with what they said were infrared goggles.

"Fascinating," one said.

"Not at all what I imagined," the other said.

"Looks like we've been overlooking something," Jack said. "No wonder Sharon liked that photo so much."

After seven hours of intense "data research," as they called it, the fifteen doctors, technicians, and forensic detectives piled back into their bus and headed back to Graceland. Jack walked them out while I calmed Chester and picked up all the rubber gloves and trash they'd left in my living room.

"They gave me this," Jack said, walking in with the large glass-encased box. "Said if we wanted to travel with the picture this would help with the structural integrity, whatever that means."

"What'd they say about all those blood tests?"

"Two or three weeks," Jack said. "I've been thinking about that."

So that's how I ended up in the green room waiting for David Letterman to call my name. Jack decided a big announcement on national TV would add an air of excitement to everything.

"This is going to be like winning the lottery," Jack said, before we boarded our plane for New York. I didn't exactly agree.

Just an hour before we boarded, I was waiting in line at an airport McDonald's when a woman came up to me with a baby bundled tightly in her arms. She just stared at me. I started feeling jittery. "Can I help you?" I said, finally.

"You're the man with Elvis, right?"

"I'm not with him," I said. "He's just in my house. I don't really have much say over it."

"Do you think you could touch my baby?" the woman asked, pushing her child toward me.

"I'm just here to get a burger," I said.

"But she's sick!" the woman shouted. People started looking.

"I'm not a doctor," I said quietly.

Tears welled up in the woman's eyes. "*The Enquirer* said a little girl with terminal cancer was cured just by standing on your front porch."

The woman was about to cry, but she looked both sad and hopeful at the same time. I've never known what to say to women when they're about to cry. Sharon used to say that was because there was no problem so big I couldn't just run away from it.

"I'm sorry," I said and put my hand on the baby's head.

I didn't tell Jack that when you win the lottery people don't throng around you hoping you can cure their diseases.

When we stepped off the plane in New York, there were camera crews and reporters and people pressed against thick velvet ropes with a bunch of beefy security guards holding them back.

"Must be some Yankees on our plane," I said.

"No," Jack said. "This is for us. For Elvis."

There had been people lining up around the house for days, folks selling T-shirts and concessions, but they were usually pretty respectful. They always said "thank you" and tried to be clean. Most everyone seemed like they were really happy they could see the picture. It was never like this. There were never old people and sick children pressed up against ropes craning to see Elvis.

"Is it true," a reporter from *Fox News* shouted, "that they have found your DNA matches the DNA found in Elvis's blood?"

"I don't think so," I said.

"But it is possible?"

"I guess," I said.

The reporter looked at me with a startled expression. I started to walk away toward baggage claim, but the reporter grabbed me by the arm. "Are you saying, Mr. Leeds, that you and Elvis may indeed share DNA?"

When I get nervous, I sometimes slip up and just say whatever I can think of to avoid an ugly situation.

"Yeah, that sounds about right," I said.

There was something close to complete silence for a moment, and Jack and I just kind of stood and stared at all the people. For a second I thought, Well, okay, time to catch the cab over to the studio. Then the people started shouting and pressing forward, and I knew I had said the wrong damn thing.

"Elvis!"

"King!"

"Touch my child! Please touch my child!"

Tony Danza finished plugging his new sitcom, and a production assistant came in and told me I was going on in five minutes, right after Jack Hanna. Then he came back and said, "I just wanted to let you know that I really believe in you. I think you've brought about a certain truth in the universe."

"I wish Chester were here," I say, after the assistant has gone. "I worry about him in a kennel."

"I think they gave those Graceland people a nicer deli platter," Jack says, peering across the hall at the other greenroom. "They sure as hell dressed better than you." I get up from the couch and took a look. The doctors wear full body HAZ-MAT suits, complete with oxygen tanks and tinted eye shields. One of them sees us staring and waves back absently.

"You think I should be worried about what the guy from *Fox News* said?" I ask. Out in the hall, one of the doctors stacks blood-filled test tubes, laptop computers and three concert posters of Elvis into a small cart and then goes back into the greenroom for a moment before stepping out with these big blown up shots of me, Jack and Chester. "I watch that show all the time," Jack says, "and they never have dependable sources. They always get these guys who talk with muffled voices and live in dark rooms."

I sit back down on the couch and try to mentally prepare myself for meeting David Letterman and finding out what the hell is bleeding out of my ex-wife's picture of Elvis. I try to imagine that I'm a fictional character, full of witty comments and neat stories, someone interesting that David Letterman might really like. I keep trying to think about the time Sonny and Cher were on the show and it was like some kind of magical experience for everyone who watched. I mean, I do have Elvis Presley bleeding in a vacuum-sealed box. And he has been changing outfits and gaining weight and getting older. I try to think about all of these things.

But I know I'm in deep trouble.

David Letterman, it turns out, is a pretty nice guy. He tells a bunch of stories about growing up an Elvis fan in Indiana, and about how he thought Mickey Mantle was cooler than Jesus when he was a kid, and so I feel real comfortable at first. The two Graceland doctors in the HAZ-MAT suits sitting next to me don't really seem to find any of this entertaining, but I do. I'm almost happy to be on TV.

All the while, Elvis is in the glass box, bleeding. He hadn't changed outfits in three days.

David Letterman himself tells me they are going to reveal the results of the blood tests right after the commercial break ends. "Are you nervous?" he asks.

"Not really," I lie. "I just want to get it over with. Get home to my dog, mostly." Dave nods like he understands exactly, but I figure he's only trying to make me feel at ease. But I'm not. I've never experienced doom firsthand, at least not until the stage manager says, "Two minutes until we're back on." It feels like someone has stuffed me into a coffin and closed the lid while I'm still alive and kicking.

"I'm not feeling too comfortable about this, Mr. Letterman," I say, but Dave is busy getting some makeup applied to his forehead.

"Forty-five seconds until we're running hot," the stage manager says.

"In fact I'm feeling like I might be sick, Mr. Letterman."

Dave smiles and pats my leg. "I feel like that all the time."

"Thirty seconds."

I look down at the picture of Elvis, and I swear to God, he looks back at me and winks. He's changed costumes and poses sometime in the last two minutes, right here on David Letterman's stage. Elvis is lying face up in a black suit with a pale red rose pinned to his lapel. He looks pretty good, all things considering. His face isn't nearly as puffy, and his skin has a sheen about it, like a porcelain doll. The only blood I can see is a single drop at the corner of his right eye.

"Fifteen seconds."

I can make out the legs and stomachs of several people gathered around the coffin. I think, and this is true, Well, at least it looks like he got some rest.

"Five. Four. Three. Two. One."

I used to get this feeling when Sharon and I were still living together—but while she was sleeping with my best friend—that my life was moving along like the clouds. Just kind of floating from here to there, no real pattern, always sort of having the sense that I wanted to go *here* now and then *there* later.

Never once during those times did I imagine *here* and *there* would end up with me sitting next to David Letterman while some doctors told me my DNA matched the DNA found in a picture of Elvis that had been crying blood on my living room wall.

"Through extensive testing," the doctors say, "we've determined that the blood found on Mr. Leeds's photo is, in fact, his own. While it remains uncertain as to how Mr. Leeds was able to perpetrate this hoax, we do know unequivocally that the blood does not belong to Mr. Presley."

"But what about all these outfit changes?" Dave say, pointing to the glass box. "Hard to explain that, isn't it?"

"It is the opinion of the Graceland Medical Advisory that Mr. Leeds simply replaced the photos himself. In short, Graceland believes that this is a shrewd and vicious infringement on the memory of Elvis Presley and in no way endorses it."

Dave keeps asking questions, but all I can do is stare at Elvis. He's changed back into the leather outfit. He is tall, skinny, handsome, and cool. And he isn't bleeding.

He kneels on the grass in front of my house on one knee, his back to the street. He wears a black baseball cap and a thick flannel shirt that he's buttoned all the way to his neck.

"Sorry," I say to the man, "but the picture stopped bleeding a month ago, and I'm late for work."

"What would you do if everywhere you went people crowded you and wanted to touch you?"

"I'd stay home," I say.

"And if one day you woke up and you were fat and ugly and didn't think you could ever be pretty again, what then?"

"I'd still have my dog, I guess."

The man laughs and bites his bottom lip like he's thinking really hard about something. "I don't think you judge a person by the audience they attract, do you?"

"No," I say. "Or by his ex-wife, I'd like to say."

"But they can make you feel important, can't they?"

"I've only got a little experience with them," I say, "but they make me feel nervous. Makes me feel like they're pulling all the air out of the sky."

"What would you do if one day all those people who lined up on your front porch came to you and said, 'You must live the rest of your life without regrets, and you must be happy.' Could you do it?"

I don't know who this guy is, but I don't mind talking to him. He's a lot nicer than those jerks on talk radio that keep saying I'm crazy.

"You want to come in and have an English muffin or something?" I ask.

"No," he says. "I've gotta run. But you didn't answer my question."

I think about it for a minute, about all the people who wanted to be near me when they thought I was performing miracles by having a bleeding rock star in my living room. I think about the way Elvis winked at me on *Late Night with David Letterman*, about how Jack told me after the show that he would always be my brother, and that all those DNA tests proved was that I might be the reincarnation of Elvis—the fact that I was born eight years *before* his death notwithstanding. And I think about that woman at McDonald's and the way she believed in me, not the picture on my wall.

"No," I say. "I'm happy right now. I don't need them to tell me."

The man takes off his baseball cap and runs his hands through a thick mane of black hair that is gray near the temples. He sucks his lips in and nods his head at me.

"You sure you don't want to come in and have some coffee or a glass of juice?" I ask. "I've got some grape soda, too."

"No," he says as a black limousine turns the corner and pulls into my driveway. "I just wanted to say that I'm glad it was you."

Some of the simplest questions are the hardest, I think. Where are you going? How are you doing? Who do you love? What makes you happy?

When are you coming back?

THE LAST TIME WE NEVER MET

B enny tells me on my second day that if I work on the job long enough, I'll begin to see a pattern. He tells me that Sundays and Mondays are suicides; Tuesdays and Thursdays, good TV nights, are natural causes; Wednesdays and Fridays, that's when people kill each other.

"What about Saturday?" I say.

"I got Saturdays off," he says. "Most people do. But come Sunday, when you start counting the hours until you gotta be back at work or you gotta go to court or you gotta get the fucking mail, right? That's when you think about checking out."

We're in the van on the way to a job, so I look down at the clipboard on my lap and check our schedule, see if Benny is right. Today is Wednesday, and we've got a suicide, two natural causes, and one undetermined.

"What's undetermined?" I ask.

Benny shakes his head. "Mummies."

I've tried to kill myself seventeen times. I've never had a near-death experience, never have seen Jesus or Jimi Hendrix beckoning me to a great white light. All that ever happens is that I come out of it alive and the world seems like a smaller, less difficult place. It's the decision making I like: who gets my CDs, who gets my car, who gets invited to the funeral, and who is expressly forbidden to mourn. In the days before I kill myself, I get my life in order.

I pay my bills, I call my ex-girlfriends, I take my dog for long walks on the beach and then feed him nothing but steak.

And when I wake up, or when the neighbor cuts me down, or when my wrists have healed and my court-imposed therapy has concluded, my world is completely reorganized. It's like filing Chapter 11.

So when we pull up in front of a two-story Brady Bunch house and the first thing I notice is how nice the lawn is—there's not a single blade higher than another and the grass is a deep forest green—and how the shrubs surrounding the house are manicured into perfect squares, I think: This is a person who got his shit together in at least one facet. When you're about to kill yourself, you take power over what you can control, and the yard is a pretty easy mark in that regard.

"Let me go inside and clear out the family," Benny says. But before he gets all the way out of the van, he stops and climbs back in. "Lemme see that clipboard for a second."

I hand him the board and for a good five minutes he reads the details of the clean, his lips moving silently.

"Don't get it," he says. "Says here the guy hung himself, but the whole house is covered in blood. How you think that happened?"

"Probably tried slitting his wrists first," I say.

"That's determination," Benny says. "Gotta admire that."

While Benny goes inside to inspect the house and review the job order, I get busy mixing up the Folex carpet cleaner and assembling the wet/dry vac. Carpet jobs are the worst: blood adheres to the microfibers in such a way that a stain you clean up today might just reappear a few days or weeks or years later. I know this because there is a stain that approximates the outline of my entire body— my fifteen-year-old body—which reappears each winter in my grandparents' Palm Springs vacation home. No matter how many times Nana scrubs the carpet, no matter how many times she has it professionally shampooed, the spot returns as soon as the air becomes moist. Every Thanksgiving my entire family gathers there for dinner and tries to ignore my dead body.

You can learn a lot about a person by looking at their refrigerator. At my house, for instance, I have a magnet from every city I've ever visited arranged geographically across the freezer section: San Francisco to Wilmington, Delaware, with pauses in the middle for places like Las Vegas, Omaha, and Springfield. I don't have anything under the magnets—no notes, no "To Do" lists, no pictures of loved ones, no recipes or cute cartoons or grocery needs.

Liam Moran, our cleanup today, has a refrigerator covered in photos. In one, he is standing in front of the entrance to Disneyland with two small children, one on either side of him. He looks happy in that way you are always happy before you go to Disneyland, before you realize that everything of value in that fantasyland costs twenty bucks or more; before you realize that you've prostituted seven hours of your inner life in a quest for make-believe happiness, false emotions, and pancakes shaped like Mickey Mouse.

"What are you doing?" Benny asks. We've been inside cleaning for a little over an hour, scrubbing the carpets and walls clean of arterial spray.

"Just looking at the pictures," I say.

"That's a bad idea," Benny says. "Soon as you think about this blood belonging to someone, it makes it personal. You don't want that."

"Why not?"

"You ever clean your toilet?"

"Sure."

"Okay. Good. Now, you don't mind cleaning up your own piss and crap. You'll get on your hands and knees all day if you got a lady coming over, right? You'll make that pot glisten. But soon as someone else drips all over it or leaves a bunch of streaks in the bowl, you wanna puke. You wanna hire someone to come in and do that job. Same thing."

I pull a picture of our dead client hugging a smiling golden retriever off the refrigerator and hand it to Benny. "Cute dog," I say.

"Gotta depersonalize that shit, my man, believe me. Or else we'll be cleaning your house next week. Serious."

The last time I didn't die was about nine months ago. I'd just been fired from my security guard job at the mall, and I felt like my entire body was covered in a virus: my scalp itched constantly, my feet were swollen, my right eye kept twitching, and my penis would get hard whenever I thought about baseball.

I Googled my symptoms and found out that I either had a brain tumor, leprosy, Lou Gehrig's disease, or severe mental problems. In even the best-case scenario, I had six months to live, and those six months would likely be filled with intense physical and/or emotional pain.

So I made my list.

1. Cancel newspaper.
2. Call Mom & Dad.
3. Throw out perishables.
4. Discard any sex toys that might make Mom & Dad uncomfortable.
5. Break up with Jill in bizarre fashion. (Maybe take a crap in her front yard?) Make her think I'm so crazy that death is actually a relief for both of us.
6. Find a kennel for Chuck.
7. Price funeral plots and coffins.
8. Rent all the movies I keep forgetting to rent.
9. Find out where Steve Mathews lives now and apologize for stealing his bike in 5th grade.
10. Purchase gun.

I looked at the word *gun*. I thought about erasing it, thought about replacing it with *Vicodin* or *twine* or even *bleach* but decided, finally, that it was time to stop fucking around. It comes down to deciding whether you're going to be a victim for the rest of your life or an actual casualty.

The next day I went to Wal-Mart and spent the better part of an afternoon walking the aisles, filling my shopping cart with all the items I'd need for my last days on earth. I bought board games like Stratego and Chutes & Ladders in case I wanted to invite my brother Frank over for a few last games. I bought a pair of new jeans and a nice collared shirt so that I could go out in something that my parents had never seen before, an outfit that didn't exist in any old Christmas or birthday snapshots, or, God forbid, home movies. There's nothing worse than popping in a wedding video and seeing the walking dead in the background: great grandparents and cousins and uncles and old friends who've died but still exist in that rummy video-taped ether of memory. I bought five packages of Oreos, three gallons of milk, duct tape, the Jimmy Buffet boxed-set, and a Beretta Bobcat pistol with eight rounds of ammo.

The essence of humanity is that people will fight to live even if all sensible logic indicates that they should really want to die. In Liam Moran's home office is a stack of letters from collection agencies, business cards from real estate agents who can save his house from foreclosure, and twenty unopened certified letters from the IRS. There's also a calendar filled out in meticulous detail that lets me know that Casey's seventh birthday is next Thursday, that Mom and Dad's anniversary is June 11, that Dr. Lewis expects to see him October 19, that his internet service is deducted automatically from his Citibank checking account on the twenty-eighth of each month, that child support is due on the thirtieth, and that this December he's taking seven days off to go fishing at Spirit Lake.

There's a fine mist of blood covering the ceiling and most of the floor, and it occurs to me that this is where it started.

I sit down in his leather executive chair and lean back, my wrists turned upward, and imagine what it must have been like to come into this room day after day knowing that the stacks of unread letters and bills were growing like a tumor, that each day that passed the tumor would mature, would become more parasitic, would begin to eat away at internal organs, would interrupt sleep, would stop up the plumbing, would eventually start calling you at your job, would attach itself to your bank account, would levy your house, and then would make you take a letter opener to your radial artery.

Slitting your wrists hurts. Most people go through their entire lives without experiencing severe pain. Sure, you'll break a toe or you'll have root canal or you'll accidentally stick your hand in a threshing machine, and all of those things are valid insofar as they are painful and leave scars and provide interesting fodder for bar stories; but actually hurting yourself to the point of death is another beast completely. Once you reach the point that you're willing to die, your body realizes certain things independent of your own desires. Start carving at your flesh with a dull object, and your skin goes into fight mode; every nerve ending starts screaming and crying and shouting and telling you that you're making a big mistake, that it's sorry for whatever it has done to you and it can all be worked out.

The thing is, most people don't want to die in pain. If you could handle pain, you'd keep living. That's why they always say people who slit their wrists, if they don't actually die in the process, are just calling attention to themselves, asking for help, pretending to be in some bad Winona Ryder movie. It's cinematic, certainly, but who really wants to spend the last moments of this mortal coil carving their skin? It's a nice starter, gets the heart pumping, but in the end it's just too much work, hurts too damn bad, and makes a mess for someone else to clean.

"Hey," Benny shouts from down the hall, "you scrubbing in there or you taking a nap? I wanna get outta here before lunch."

I get out of Liam's chair, set up the extension ladder, and get to work on the ceiling.

My girlfriend Jill seemed to know something was wrong the moment she stepped into my apartment. She worked at Wicks-n-Sticks in the same mall I'd been fired from, so she knew how much different candles cost and knew that I didn't have a lot of money to waste on them.

"Did you get these at Pottery Barn?" she asked. I'd invited her over for dinner and had spent a ridiculous amount of time setting up pretty candles all over the dining room, down the hall, and into the bedroom. It looked very sweet and romantic except that in the bedroom I'd set up an intricate shrine to Cher, complete with Photoshopped pictures of the three of us locked in romantic embraces. I wanted to leave Jill with a real impression, something she could blame the rest of her life on if it all turned to shit after my death. It wasn't her fault that I was being attacked by aggressive tumors, disease, and madness, and I wanted to make sure she had every excuse not to blame herself. She was only nineteen and already an assistant manager—a real woman with a future.

"I did," I said. "Just for you."

Jill ran her hand along the smooth silo-shaped blue candle I'd placed on the center of the kitchen table. "It's all the same products as Wicks-n-Sticks. Pottery Barn just uses more expensive packing," she said. "I could have gotten you thirty-five percent off if you'd told me ahead of time."

I came up behind her and kissed her softly on the nape of her neck. I'll miss that, I thought. I'll miss the way goose bumps rise along Jill's arms whenever I kiss her for the first time on any given day. I'll miss the late-night telephone calls where she reads me her bad rhyming poetry. I'll miss the way she always smells vaguely like burning wax.

When I'm dead tomorrow, I thought, and looking down on creation with Karen Carpenter, I imagine I'll consider Jill the one person who could have saved me had she but known the depths of my various illnesses. If nothing else, Jill will be remembered as my single most memorable mall-based relationship, after the girl I dated from Hot Dog on a Stick.

"Stop," Jill said, squirming away from me.

"I'm sorry," I said. "I like the way your neck feels."

"Look," she said, "I can't stay."

No, I thought. No. No. You don't get to do this. You. Do. Not. Get. To. Kill. Me.

"Sure you can," I said. "I have something very important to show you in the bedroom. We can skip dinner even."

"I'm real busy at work right now," Jill said. "And with the holidays coming up I know things will be hair ball for, like, the next three months. Which is totally not fair to you."

Jill kept talking but I couldn't hear her. My mind was flooded alternately with images of her sobbing at my funeral, her face buried in my mother's shoulder, and then, sixty years later, dressed in the same outfit she wore the day I died, placing roses on my grave.

"I'm dying," I said.

"I know it hurts," Jill said, "but we can totally still be friends. Maybe our relationship wasn't meant to leave the mall, you know? Like how actors and actresses fall in love when they make a movie together, but when the movie stops filming, they're, like, not at all in love anymore."

"No," I said. "I mean I have a tumor. There's something wrong with my blood. I'll be dead in six months."

"You're sweet," she said, "but I'm not into you." Jill took my face in her hands, kissed me once on the forehead, and walked out of my apartment.

Benny tells me that Liam Moran didn't bother to leave a note.

"Is that normal?" I ask. I'm holding the ladder while Benny sands the friction stains out of the cross beam Liam finally hung himself from. People don't usually use actual rope to hang themselves; it's just not all that convenient when you think about it. Very few people know how to tie a noose, for one; and for two, most people don't have a non-lethal reason to have rope sitting around the house. Liam fastened several leather belts together, hence the marks.

"Majority of suicide victims, if they're any kind of decent, will leave word. Way I understand it now, lotta people do it via email," Benny says. "You know how you can schedule mail to go out at a specific time? I heard about a lady who done it so her husband got an email from her every day for a year, calling him names and blaming him for shit. Now that's wrong, you wanna know my opinion." Benny applies a dash of rubbing alcohol to a rag and works over two deep smudges until they disappear. "You see how I did that?" he asks.

I nod.

"That won't work on a rope burn. Best bet is cheap hairspray in that case. Something like Aqua Net works best." Benny climbs down the ladder and surveys his work from below. When he's satisfied, he tells me to get up and inspect it as well.

From atop the ladder, I see the entire world as Liam Moran saw it last. I see that the sun cuts across his two leather couches and settles on the face of his television. I see that water damage has begun to stain the south-facing wall and that Liam hung picture frames to hide the creeping yellow blight, but that he never filled them with real pictures, leaving instead the hollowed-out smiles and faked exuberance of cut-out families. I take a step down, to where I imagine Liam must have hung, and come face to face with the center photograph of the largest frame. It's of a man and a woman running down a beach, their footprints perfectly placed behind them. A big gold dog churns up sand beside them, and a setting sun can be seen on the horizon; which means the last people Liam Moran saw didn't even really exist to him.

I scan every other vantage point Liam might have had, looking for one thing he might have settled on instead, one final image that might have made him happy, his own mental suicide note, but I find absolutely nothing. His coda was merely his hanging body.

"What you see up there is attention to detail," Benny is saying. "Lotta cleaners, including other folks at the company, they wouldn't even have thought to get up there to decontaminate that beam. But I think about the family, know what I'm saying? They know that's where he spent his last moments alive, so they're gonna spend time looking at it. They see something out of the ordinary, shit, that'll turn them upside down. If I can help relieve that future burden, I figure I should try. That's one lesson you should take."

I descend the ladder and stand beside Benny, who is still admiring his work. He takes a deep breath, exhales, and his whole body relaxes.

"Have you ever thought about killing yourself, Benny?" I ask.

"Nope," Benny says. "You know why?"

"Fear?"

"Naw, fuck that," Benny says. "I'm not scared of shit. You kill yourself and for the rest of time people only remember that you were crazy. I believe in God and all that good shit, go to church on Sunday if my wife makes me, but that doesn't mean as much to me as leaving a decent legacy for my kids. Who wants to be the son of some crazy motherfucker? Know what I'm saying?"

I tell him that I do but in truth I don't. Suicide has always seemed to me to be the sheerest sign of sanity: if you know that the rest of your life is going to be an utter waste —if you have tangible proof—why not end it before the pain and suffering become so acute that you're driven mad by it? Stay sane and die by your own rules, and the only people who will think you're crazy are the ones who can't see how easy it would be for them to do the same.

Benny and I gather up our supplies and start loading them back into the van. It's taken us four hours, but we've managed to scrub the walls and floors free of blood (there wasn't all that much, really), replaced the ventilation filter on the air conditioning to help with the recurring smells of both dead and living Liam (this isn't part of a standard clean, and in fact Benny doesn't even charge for it; it's something he alone does—he even buys the filters himself), and removed the friction marks from the hanging. All that's left is for the family to sign off on our work. Benny checks his watch.

"They should be here in a few minutes," he says. "Think I can trust you to do the closing paperwork?"

"I don't know," I say. "Do you trust me?"

Benny smiles for the first time all day, and I think that he's been trying to suss out the answer to that question since the moment he met me.

"I like you," Benny says. "You're a little crazy, though, huh?"

"A little," I say.

"A lotta people get into this line of work because they're ghouls or fucking kleptos, but you're not like that. I can see that plain enough by the scars on your arms."

"I've got scars in other places," I say. I unbutton the collar of my shirt and yank it down a few inches.

Benny cocks his head and leans forward to take a closer look. "Well, shit," he says. "Rope?"

"Nylon twine."

"How long ago?"

"Which time?"

Before Benny can answer, the front door opens and the entire Moran family comes walking in. Mom and Dad are dressed like they're going to a business luncheon, except that their bodies are slumped from the waist up. Ex-wife is still wearing her wedding ring, or maybe she just has it on in memory of her dead ex, or maybe they got divorced because he was a suicidal maniac who was a threat to the kids. The kids. A boy and a girl. They smell like vomit and maple syrup and will live the rest of their lives with the thought that they might have been the cause of this, because that's what children often do—at least until they get old enough to realize that anyone with an ATM card is about one bad day away from taking the same route.

"I'll handle this," Benny says under his breath. "Best if you wait outside."

I waited three days after Jill walked out on me before I actually tried to kill myself. During those three days, I made sure Jill knew I wasn't missing her. I called her and told her I understood her motivations and then took her out for a "state of the break-up" lunch where we talked about all the things we hated about each other as mates but that would probably be tolerable if we were just friends, and then decided to be just that. Jill even fixed me up on a date with her manager, a forty-year-old woman named Maggie who'd been working at Wicks-n-Sticks for seventeen years. Maggie and I decided on a Japanese table-cooking place for the following week, which was great because by the time that date rolled around I'd be dead.

I prepared to die on a Thursday. I woke up early, ate a big breakfast, took several laxatives so I'd be able to rid myself without doing it in my pants as soon as rigor hit, sent off my last set of bills, and then sat down to write my note.

Dear Mom & Dad,

This isn't about you. Not this time. I've found out that I'm dying from a serious unnamed ailment and do not wish to live the duration of my life mired in pain. You'll find that my estate is in order and that Chuck is in that dog spa on 11th Street; same as last time. He's paid for through next week, so you might as well let him live it up a bit. He deserves it. He's been a good friend all these long years and I'd hate for him to see me like this. As for my funeral, I have a couple specific requests:

1. *Jill shouldn't come. Trust me. She never loved me.*
2. *I'd like the Jimmy Buffet boxed-set to be played during the duration of the service. You'll find it on my bed next to the suit I'd like to be buried in.*
3. *I'd prefer the service to be non-religious. It's already too late.*
4. *I've attached a list of cemeteries nearby and the prices for different kinds of coffins. Please do not go overboard on this.*

I love you both very much. I'm sorry for the trouble I've caused you and for all the times you've had to find me near-dead. It was silly, wasn't it? All that time I spent trying to kill myself and, in the end, it was disease that finally claimed me. Or, at least, made me kill myself for real. You were good parents and I wish I'd appreciated you more while I was still alive.

Love,

Your Son Bobby

I noticed when I was done that I hadn't mentioned any of my siblings. I thought about rewriting the note to include a few bons mots meant for them, but decided that they never really knew me anyway, that I'd spent several other suicide notes saying exactly how I felt about them and they'd always used those notes against me later. So fuck them. I gave the letter a precise Z fold and placed it into a cream-colored envelope on the coffee table.

After spending another thirty minutes canceling my cable TV and cell phone service and covering the floor with plastic tarps, I placed duct tape over my eyes (to keep them from popping out from the force of the gun blast—I'm a donor), picked up my gun, and shot myself in the head.

When I woke up in the hospital, my mother and father were sitting beside my bed reading magazines as if they were waiting for a pizza to be delivered and didn't want to get invested in a TV program.

"How did I get here?" I asked.

My mother didn't bother to look up from her reading. "Ambulance."

"I should be dead," I said.

My dad set his magazine down and got up from his seat so he could pace in front of my bed. He used to be in the military so he finds it useful to pace while he speaks, like he is addressing a line of stoic young men poised for battle. "Son," my dad said, "you're crazy. I've accepted that. Your mother has begun to accept that.

What you're *not* is sick. The nice thing about wanting to die is that if you are patient and wait long enough, it will eventually happen. Until that time, I have just one request."

My dad stopped pacing and stood directly in front of me, trying to make eye contact. It was hard because I was still blinking from the lights and trying to make sense of how it was that I wasn't having this conversation via the Ouija board. "What's that, Dad?"

"Put a cork in this suicide business," Dad said. "You're goddamn awful at it—a terrible failure, really—and every time you run off and shoot a hole in your head or stab yourself in the chest, I end up dipping into my retirement just to keep you alive. Mother and I would like to live in comfort from here on out and this has been a tremendous tax on us."

This seemed reasonable enough, and I said so. Dad sat back down beside Mom and resumed reading.

"How long have I been out?" I asked.

"Three days," Mom said.

"Do I have a tumor anywhere?"

"No, honey," Mom said.

"What about that baseball player disease?"

"Clean," Mom said. "Other than a good chunk of missing scalp, you're in lovely shape."

Beside my bed were literally hundreds of scented candles, cute get well cards, and a music box that, when I opened it, played "I Got You Babe" by Sonny & Cher.

Cher.

Shit.

"Has Jill been by?"

"Every day," Mom said. "They even let her sleep beside you last night. You two looked so sweet together this morning."

The three of us remained silent until the doctor arrived to check my vitals and tell me how lucky I was, that I could have ended up much, much worse. Yes, I told him, I am so very lucky. I could be dead.

"Jesus Christ," Benny says. He's sitting behind the wheel of the van but hasn't started it yet. "You see those kids?"

"They smelled funny."

"Yeah," Benny says, "I noticed that. Why bring them to the house? What good does that do for them?"

"Closure?"

"Little kids don't know shit about closure," Benny says. "I got an eight-year-old who visits his fucking hamster's grave every morning before school and every afternoon when he gets back. That rodent's been dead for three years. Three years! You believe that? So don't tell me about closure."

Benny reaches into the glove box and pulls out a handkerchief and blows his nose. "I hate this fucking job," Benny says flatly. "Gotta depersonalize this shit. I keep saying that."

I stare at Benny and try to figure out what to say next, but when he starts crying, really sobbing, I just sit there silently and watch.

Liam Moran's front door opens and those two ill-smelling children step out. They've changed into shorts and T-shirts—clothes I recognize from photos on the refrigerator, clothes they must have kept at the house for custody weekends—and the tallest of them, the girl, disappears around the side yard. The boy stands in the middle of the perfect lawn and stares at me with an unblinking intensity that makes me feel embarrassed. I think that he sees something in my face that looks familiar, something that reminds him of his dead father or of his living father or of the moments when he imagines how much easier his own life might be if it wasn't, if it just failed to be. But then the lawn erupts in a rainbow of sprinklers, and the girl reappears, and the two of them run and jump and smile and laugh and his face looks just like a child's, just like anyone's, and before I even notice, Benny has put the van into drive and we are pulling away, heading toward another clean, and those kids have already begun to shrink into another life.

The first time I tried to kill myself, I stuck my head in the oven and nearly set my head on fire. I was twelve. When my mother found me there on the floor a few minutes later, my hair a singed nest, the kitchen filled with the acrid smell of gas and burnt flesh, she lay down beside me and held my hand and cried and told me how much she loved me; how we'd all be together in Heaven; how I was safe now from whatever made me so sad and angry. I don't think she knew I was alive. I don't think she ever knew.

TRY NOT TO LOSE HER

Hear your father's story about pouring salt on snails when he was your age and then hearing his own father say, *The boy's not right, you know? How is he ever gonna find a wife?* Wonder why he tells the story at all. Search the attic until you find the box marked YEARBOOKS. See your dad staring out at you in his freshman year, face like the surface of a Wheat Thin, expression blank and sullen. Think of him looking a bit like a turnip. Know that you look a lot like him.

Sit on the grass while your parents drink lemonade on a fuming July day. They discuss you in some kind of code. "We should get his thyroid checked. Maybe it's medical." "No, morbidly obese is not accurate. Because I say so, that's why." "By fifteen, he should be out of any stages, agreed?" Hate them with a passion usually reserved for Allen Jervis, the kid across the street that beats you up because you're fat. Run inside and find the box of Ex-Lax you stole from the drugstore. Swallow three tablets. Lay flat on your stomach on the cool bathroom floor. Press down. Wait for action.

On the way to Safeway with your best friend, John, feel guilty for touching your penis the night before. Consider telling him, despite the enormous guilt, that it felt pretty darn good. Think about that again as your ten-speed goes over a bump and you almost lose a testicle. Laugh at the fat woman in line in front of you, even though you have a Rocky Road, a Snickers, two Butterfingers, and a pack of Hubba Bubba in your hand. Act interested when John tells you that he's been studying for the PSAT because he's going to take the Bar exam someday and all the preparation needs to begin at an early age. Tell John that a future in textiles is in the works for you. You aren't quite sure what textiles are, actually, but it shuts John the fuck up long enough for you to enjoy your candy.

Start picturing Her. Chestnut hair. Green eyes. Not a normal combination of attributes, granted, but you've seen it before in old pulp novels, so it must exist. A femme fatale from an old Raymond Chandler novel would work fine. Decide that She doesn't care about weight or looks or your bizarre family. She's above that. Work hard at your indifference to Her. She wants you, remember. The chase, man, all girls love the chase. Imagine how you will seduce Her. You've always liked necks, so you start there. Let your tongue dart around Her clavicle. Hold Her throat gently. She likes it, so move south.

Try again with indifference. Stay north until you're more experienced with your imagination.

Think about wearing better clothes. Throw away all your heavy metal T-shirts, ripped jeans, and Chuck Taylors. See yourself riding a Harley with Her on the back, hair flowing behind you. People in the other cars watch you two and can't stop wondering what they did wrong with their own lives. Listen to Johnny Cash albums. No, fuck that. Read about being a transcendentalist. Dabble in existentialism. She'll like that. Read a lot of Emerson. Give of yourself. But not too much. She'll like a mystery, so keep the Johnny Cash albums, too.

John thinks you're getting loopy. Screw him. Go on a diet for Her, even though She wouldn't care. Make new friends. Hang out with Gus and Jared. Smoke cloves because it gives you an edge. Consider that wherever She is, She's thinking about you, trying to figure out why you haven't found her yet. Rent *The Wizard of Oz* and watch it with the sound off. Listen to Pink Floyd in the background. Feel like She's with you in the room, and She's digging it.

Close the door. Move south on yourself.

Become so thin that you bruise easily. Eavesdrop on your mother while she's on the phone. "There's no rule that says boys can't be anorexic. He does look better, doesn't he?" Crank call John five times a day. Find out from a friend that John's folks are seriously thinking about pressing charges. Act unaffected. Get call blocking from AT&T for another dollar a month. Your parents will never notice. Boredom is your friend. When Thanksgiving rolls around, pretend not to care. Say you're making a stand for Squanto, the first oppressed American. Tell your Uncle Steve that he's an asshole for calling you one of those kids he's scared of in the mall. Swallow a couple laxatives. Feel better.

Ask girls out. Practice, you know, so you're ready. Use corny lines on the ones who actually say yes. Mention their shoes. Use so much Oxy-10 Cover Formula on your face that you look like Michael Jackson post-op. Wear bad aftershave just to see if the girls notice, or if they are really into you for what you bring to the table. Park your car at a park, and ask them to play on the swings with you. They'll laugh, think you're cute, boyish, non-threatening. Make your move when they are laughing. Practice tongue kissing. She'll be into that. Practice how you'll describe the ones who won't go out with you. Settle on, "A couple clowns short of a circus."

Act like a family friend at your mom's funeral. Cry, because a friend would cry. Indifference is the key. Apologize to your Uncle Steve; it was his sister, you know? Skip the wake. Sit in your room and listen to The Cure. Think how it's too bad that you didn't believe her when she said it felt like her appendix was bursting; too bad your father had to go off on a business trip that very day.

After everyone leaves, sit in the kitchen with your dad and cry with him. *She* can wait. Give the man some solace. It was his wife, you know?

The new girl from Tennessee sits next to you in homeroom. She wears a tiny skirt that highlights her tanned thighs. Volunteer to show her around the campus. Watch John seethe. He's still playing D&D and board games, and you're escorting a babe around the high school. Gus and Jared give you a thumbs up. Tell her where the cool kids eat lunch, though you aren't considered a cool kid. Show her where you eat lunch instead. Listen while she tells you how sad she is. How much she misses Tennessee. "California is so different," she says.

Ask her out for Friday night. Pick her up twenty minutes late. Don't apologize. Tell her you want to go to the discount theater because they are playing the entire original *Star Wars* trilogy back-to-back-to-back. She says that would great. She loves Boba Fett.

This may be Her.

Try to unhook her bra in the back seat of your Nissan Sentra. Solving a Rubik's Cube in the dark would be easier. Yank her shoulder straps down, like they do in the movies. "Hey!" she says. "You ripped my bra." Say nothing. Kiss her clavicle. "Asshole!" she says. "You ripped my fucking bra and you're choking me." Tell her that she's the one, baby, she's the one. Tell her you've been priming for this moment all your life.

Tell Gus she's a couple clowns short of a circus.

Wake up your dad and tell him that you are graduating at seven o'clock. He smiles. He looks dead. He smells like flat Sprite. "Are you valedictorian?" Make the guy happy. Sure, Dad, you tell him, sure. Dad goes back to sleep.

Tell your dad you'll write. Make sure he has paid your tuition. Tell him that you're okay if he starts dating, that at some point he has to start over, make some choices. Don't tell him that your counselor at school told you to tell him this; or that you confided in your counselor that things at home were rotten, like they were physically rotting; or that you feel like you've been swallowed by something black and formless that, you think, emanates from the closed door to the storage closet, where your mother's ashes sit locked in a box.

Join a fraternity and get drunk for an entire year. Look for Her in the halls, at parties, sorority mixers. Come up with a lot of girls who look like Her, who are not Her. Amend wish list to include the following: witty, big breasts, olive skin tone, off-campus housing.

Robin is all of the above. Fuck her on the clean Formica of

her off-campus apartment kitchen. Touch her breasts while she sleeps just because you can. Drink Ovaltine in the morning with her. Laugh at her milk mustache. Say, Let's skip class. Let's just do it all day. She tells you she loves your body, your thin stomach and tight biceps. She asks, "How many laxatives do you take a day?"

Think of yourself as the uncaring man you are. Practice boredom again. Act indifferent. Pay attention to her faults. Ask her if she thinks that cottage cheese on her ass will clear up.

Go to the health center for a cold compress; find out Robin broke your jaw. Strong girl. Drink dinner through a straw for a month. Call your dad and tell him you need help paying the hospital bill. He says that he's not feeling like a man anymore. He says, "When your mom died I should have died, too." Tell him he's important. It comes out sounding like *impotent*. He hangs up. Listen to the dial tone until you can't differentiate between it and your own breathing.

Fly home. Your dad is sitting at the kitchen table looking at a scrapbook. Tell him you were worried about him. Notice the stacks of dirty dishes in the sink. Remember how your mom designated every Sunday "cleaning day." When your dad falls asleep on the couch, wash all the dishes. Vacuum his bedroom. Throw out three weeks' worth of newspapers.

Sit next to a girl from your college on the plane home. She talks to you for the entire flight. She's had an abortion. She loved a guy who really screwed her over. She wears a scarf around her neck that is covered with butterflies. Notice she has a butterfly charm around her neck. Tell her you've always loved the word *mariposa*. Go back to her off-campus apartment and watch game shows until four in the morning. Wake up with her head on your chest. Evaluate the situation. Go through her CD collection. Find that she has a Neil Diamond CD and also a Notorious B.I.G. CD. Check her refrigerator. Note the abundance of Tupperware. Check out her body again. Wake her with a soft kiss to the cheek. Tell her, through your wired jaw, that she is beautiful.

At your fraternity house, cops are parked three deep on the front lawn. See your buddy Trent being carried out in handcuffs, wearing your shoes. Five drug-sniffing German shepherds are canvassing the rooms. Sit in your car listening to the soundtrack from *Pulp Fiction*.

Sit in Starbucks with your frat brothers Bill and Dylan and lament the situation. It's fucked, man, you say. "Fucked," Dylan says and points out the barista. "Pretty hot, huh?" Walk up to the counter, eyes steady on her, mouth snarled into a half smile. Look dangerous. Look like a guy to fall in love with. Her name is Mandy. She's a junior majoring in English.

Stay at Mandy's off-off-campus house playing Scrabble and Monopoly with her housemates, both English majors, too. Tell them that you've been working on some poetry yourself. When they hand you paper and pencil and ask you to write something right now for them, write about your mother's face. Watch the girls watching you. One of the girls, Lisa, is a grad student. She says there are hints of Carver and Auden in your work.

Forget about Mandy. Go to bed with Lisa.

Lisa wants to tie you up and do some role-playing. Agree. She is here to save you. She already has. Wake up in the morning with rope grooves in your wrists and small burns all over your chest and belly from candle wax. Your groin is sticky with dried honey.

The girl from the plane calls you a month later. She thinks she is pregnant. Tell her you don't have the time to listen to that noise, you're going to be a featured reader at an open mic poetry reading. To get back in the mood, you put on a Jane's Addiction CD and listen to "Mountain Song" at decibels that make your eardrums ache.

Stand up there wearing all black. You are Indifference. You are Nothingness. You could be dead, but dead doesn't seem like such a good deal anymore. Dead is dead, and dead is not cool. Stillness. Nirvana. Adjust the mic down to your level. See Lisa in the crowd. Think about how last night she just wouldn't stop fucking you. She didn't want to eat. She poured orange juice on your legs and lapped it up like a dog. You freestyled some poetry on her while she did things with a big purple monstrosity called *Mr. Whistle*. She doesn't wash her sheets because she says she wants your smell. *I love your old skin.* Read your poetry for Lisa. Let the words fall out of your mouth and shatter in the air. They all snap. They snap for you.

Dream you are on stage playing the guitar. The girl from the plane is giving birth on your amp, and Lisa is the midwife. Wake up next to Lisa. She's got on your black T-shirt, and she's snoring out of her mouth. Remember the way she told you how proud she was of you after the poetry reading. Think about the way she kisses with her tongue. Evaluate the way you have "normal" sex with her. Consider the fact that she is nice, smart, witty, pretty, has chestnut brown hair, and green eyes (okay, brown, but with a green tint to them).

Change your phone number. Tell everyone except the girl from the plane. Make an effort to forget her name. Move half your stuff into Lisa's place. Drop out of the fraternity. Poets don't belong to fraternities.

Find out from friends at home that your dad has been seen wandering the streets at night. Listen to a book of poetry driving home. Nearly fall asleep from boredom. Who reads this pretentious shit? Play a CD of songs Lisa made that remind her of you. Try to figure out how Bruce Springsteen's "The River" applies to you. Knock on the front door of your childhood home because you've lost the key you used to wear around your neck. Your dad opens the door and hugs you, squeezes you, says, "I missed you." Stay the weekend.

Dad says, "You don't know how much you love someone until you realize you never told them. I'm not making sense, I know." He says, "You have her eyes. You have her lips and her ears. You even have her fingers." Call Lisa and find her out of breath. Ask her what she's doing. "I ran in from the garage to get the phone," she says. You've been in that garage. Can't hear a damn thing from there.

Call your Uncle Steve and ask him about your dad. "He's just skin," Uncle Steve says. "It's like he's lost all his connective tissue. And I think he needs to be medicated. Lithium maybe." Call him an asshole and hang up. Go with your father to Target to get a couple of lamps for the house. Buy him lunch at Chili's and tell him you think he should see a doctor. Your dad agrees. "I'll do it on Monday," he says. Tell him about your poetry and about Lisa. Say, She's the one, Dad. Drive back to school.

Spend the night at Lisa's. Make every part of her body verse. Touch her navel with your tongue and draw your finger over her lips. Tell her for the first time that you love her. Hold her face close to yours; say it over and over again: "I love you." After she goes to sleep, notice a bite mark on her neck. You never bite her neck. You bite her shoulder, never her neck.

See the girl from the plane at Borders. Hide in the café. Feel nauseous. She is wearing stretch pants. Ask the clerk what she purchased after you're sure she's left the store. Two books, *A Single Mother's Guide to Parenthood* and *Seven Steps to Healthy Abs After Pregnancy*, and one movie, *Steel Magnolias*.

Lisa becomes really interested in soccer and starts listening to rap music. You see her wearing an awful lot of athletic gear: sweat pants, biking shorts, and sports bras. She says that her love for you just keeps growing. She's tutoring a guy from the soccer team who's getting his minor in literature. Try to imagine your life without Lisa. Could you live? How long would you binge on food? Could you marry someone else? Touch Lisa's hand. It is cold. There is grass in her hair.

Call Lisa when she says she won't be home. Hang up when she answers.

Go to your father's funeral on a rainy Sunday in June. Mull over the warning signs. Sort out the reasons why you couldn't save him—not that you possess a cure for cancer or the power to make your father visit a doctor, even when anyone could plainly see something was eating him alive. Remember that black force from your childhood. Realize that you can't feel it anymore. That you haven't felt it in years. That you were never scared of it, but that you always sensed it was there; that it was calling; that it was coming; that all you had to do was accept it and it would be yours.

Sit in your old house and listen to your neighbors tell you what a fine family you were. *Were.* After everyone has left, go through the cabinet you were never allowed to go through. Sticky letters, dried flowers, mementos from trips to Disneyland and Lake Tahoe, a receipt from a hotel room in Medford, Oregon. Spread everything out in front of you and recreate your parents' courtship. In one picture, your parents stand on the edge of a long dock surrounded by young kids, but then you understand that your parents are just young kids, too, that they are only a few years older than you. You never knew these people. You knew your parents, but not these people. Your mother is tan, and her hair is long and blond, and your father holds her around the waist, his fingers dug deep into her flesh, holding on. Always holding on. He could never let go.

Touch your father's clothes. Smell him in the folds of the blanket you drape around yourself. Play back the messages on his answering machine. Hear your own voice echoing through the kitchen: "Are you there? Dad? Are you there?"

Call Lisa and listen to the phone ring forty-seven times. Imagine her dead in a ditch. Imagine her and Soccer Boy pouring hot wax on each other. Throw up. Consider running outside with your father's favorite blanket wrapped around your shoulders, screaming. Lie flat on the bathroom floor. Put a laxative in your mouth. Spit it out. Be a man. Grow up. No more stages. Call Lisa again. Again. Again.

Wonder why Mandy is so happy to see you when you show up at the house unannounced a week later. Open Lisa's bedroom door and see her straddling Soccer Boy. When she says, "This doesn't mean I don't love you," tell her that her math is all screwed up. Threaten Soccer Boy with bodily harm and extreme impudence to his corpse. Don't even take into consideration that Soccer Boy is six-foot-three and 195 pounds of lean muscle mass. He's in no position right now to do anything. Go into Lisa's kitchen and break all of her dishes. Scream that you hate her poetry.

Run into the mother of your child at the grocery store. You are buying beer, and she is buying something for her queasy stomach. Tell her that you are ready to take a role in this. Say that although you've made some mistakes in life, you are trying to right your ship. Say all the important words: *Lie. Us. Regret. Karma. My Father Died Of Cancer A Week Ago Because He Never Went To The Doctor, Not Once, Not Even When It Must Have Been Terribly Painful Just To Be, You Know? It Must Have Hurt Just To Be Alive.* Watch her break down and cry in the frozen foods section. She says that her life is completely unglued. "I'm not even sure if it's yours," she says.

Give up poetry. Who writes this pretentious shit? Consider textiles. Consider permanence. Consider looking up your old friend John. Call your Uncle Steve and say, With mom and dad gone we've only got each other. "You're an asshole," he says, and hangs up.

Run into Lisa at the student union. Uncomfortable silence. Ask about the condition of your favorite black T-shirt. Apologize for that remark about her poetry. You know how fragile she is about her talent. Laugh at an old inside joke you share. Go back to her place and fuck like there is no tomorrow, because there isn't one with Lisa. Tell her you would have married her, had children, grown old. Describe the box of keepsakes you found at your parents' house. Wonder what kind of keepsakes the two of you would have stored away. *Mr. Whistle* and some twine? Find your favorite black T-shirt rolled up in a ball on the floor. Pick it up on your way out the door.

Call the mother of what may be your child. Her name is Kelly. Use it. Say, "Kelly, let's get a blood test."

Punch your old friend John's name into Google and find a news story about him. He murdered his college astronomy teacher for failing him. Your old friend John is doing life at San Quentin.

Listen to soft music and wait for Kelly to come pick you up. Think about Her. Not Kelly. Her. Reconsider the model. Make some changes. Fine-tune the picture. Get a call from your Uncle Steve. He says, "Family is family is family." Make plans to fly up to San Francisco to see him. Remember that day in July when you were fifteen. Realize you don't know where to begin. Consider that time is moving around you, people are filtering through you. Live.

MYTHS OF OUR TIME

I was fourteen when I saw the Loch Ness monster, and though in the years since I've come to believe that monsters do not exist, that in fact monsters and people and ghosts and Jesus are all as likely to be unreal as real, I do know that what I saw *was* and *is*. It's probable that what I witnessed was not a monster at all; that beneath its sheen of slick black skin, beyond its forked tail and sharp yellow eye, down deep below the surface of the water, it was just another being. Another object. Who we are, how we are perceived, is like most things: a confluence of events, a trick of memory.

It was the summer of 1985, which was memorable for also being the first summer without my sister Gina. That January, on her sixteenth birthday, she jumped off the Golden Gate Bridge and drowned, or, more likely, broke her neck or broke her back or suffered a traumatic brain injury and *then* drowned. We'd never know for sure because we wouldn't actually get her body back for another six months, and when we did it wasn't much body at all. In a box about the size of a cheap valise, the county coroner sent us Gina's left arm and her Swatch watch (the black one with French words for numbers) and a short letter explaining all the pertinent information—genetic results and the like—and a photo of where her arm had washed up.

It had been on the news, of course, as the appearance of an arm on the shores of the Pacific is often a cause for concern, and for a time I reveled in it. Teachers, friends, strangers on the street who'd seen our family on TV would stop me and tell me how sorry they were, how tragic it all was, how young Gina was, how I should appreciate every moment of life as if it were my last, which eventually made it all the more sad: I didn't want to live my life for Gina's remembrance and I didn't want to live like every split second was potentially my last.

Gina was dead and that was enough. Before she leapt to her death, she managed to type out a detailed will, replete with smudges of Wite-Out and smiley faces written in the margins, that said she'd decided sixteen years were enough time to be alive, which is sad and catastrophic and a lie. She said she wanted her ashes scattered along Loch Ness. She said that she wanted me and Dad and Mom to have a nice vacation in Scotland and to think of her whenever we saw someone happy. And then like a senior would in a yearbook she'd never own, she left her friends memories: *Kara gets that night on the fifty-yard line with Matt Caswell. Stacy gets the twelve pack of Natty Light and the Cheez-Its and long talks in the Camaro. Brian gets nothing he hasn't already had! J/K! Luv ya, Brian!* And that was it: Gina was dead. Gina was an arm. Gina was a Swatch watch and a newscast and three airline tickets to Scotland and a box of ashes on my father's lap.

"I'm not sure what we're supposed to do," Dad said. The three of us stood on the shore of Loch Ness and stared out over the rippling gray water and watched boats filled with tourists ferry back and forth to a short dock a few hundred yards away. Beside us, a Japanese tour group huddled around a tall woman with flaming red hair and watched intently as she held up large photos of the Loch Ness monster as seen from the very vantage point they currently held. Every few moments, a collective "Oh!" rose up from the people and then subsided into murmurs and whispers in both English and Japanese. *Could it be? Sa. Sa.*

"Maybe you should say some words," Mom said.

"Yes," Dad said. "But after that? Do we put the ashes in the water? Or do we let them go into the air? I guess we've never talked about this. What do you think, Scott?"

"Isn't there a way we could do both?" I said.

"All right." My dad nodded. "All right. Let's hold hands then."

The three of us clasped hands—me to my mother, my mother to my father—and then Dad cleared his throat, and when I thought he was about to speak, when I thought he was going to finally say whatever he'd been trying to say for all the years I'd known him, all the years Gina knew him, maybe all the years our mother knew him, he instead began to sob uncontrollably.

One of the Japanese tourists, a man of about sixty, walked over and handed my father a handkerchief when it became clear my father was not going to stop crying anytime soon.

"Thank you," Dad said after he caught his breath. "I'm sorry if I'm making a scene here. We're trying to carry out our daughter's last wishes." When the man didn't respond, Dad paused for a moment, looked at me with an expression I'd not seen previously—something between sadness and honest guilt—and repeated what he'd said, though this time he said it in Japanese, a language I didn't know he knew.

So many secrets have passed between my father and me since that day. You'd think I could figure out the importance of one detail over another detail. I'm still not sure why he chose to break that first barrier between who I believed he was and who he actually might have been, but his words flowed like they'd always been his that day; a fluency of thought and emotion he rarely possessed, no matter that his words were in a language I did not understand.

"Oh," the man said mournfully. He turned from my father then, took my mother's hands in his, and patted them gently. "*Hai. Hai. Kanashimi ni michita.*" He then regarded me with a slight bow and passed me a tissue, too.

"Let's not do this today," Dad said after the man left us. "Let's go back to our hotel and have lunch and forget about it all for one more day."

"Jeff," my mother said to my father, "we can't simply keep doing this."

My father was a spy. My father was an assassin. My father worked for NASA or the NSA or the CIA. Or he knew who killed whom and where they were buried. Or maybe he was none of those things. I've not known that particular answer. I will not know; or I will. Lives have become declassified over the years as the world has changed, so maybe one day I'll get the exact truth. Until then, I know this: He woke up every morning, ate breakfast with Gina and me, drove us to school, and then went to his office; except we never saw his office. And sometimes, he drove us to school, went to his office, and then didn't come home for two days or two weeks or, once, six months. There'd be no advance warning. We'd get home from school and our mom would be sitting at the kitchen table with a cake or a pie or a cheese casserole on a platter in front of her.

"Your father had to go out of town on business," she'd say. Sometimes her face would be streaked with old tears, her careful makeup marred and cracked. At first, we were told our father was a pilot. Then, later, when we were slightly older—around the time *Raiders of the Lost Ark* came out—he said he was an archaeologist. Eventually, we just didn't discuss it.

"When is he coming back?" Gina would ask.

"You know, Gina," Mom would say.

"I really don't."

"Please just be the person I need you to be, okay, Gina?"

"Who sent the cake?" I'd ask.

"Mrs. Graham," Mom would say. Or: "Mrs. Jones." Or: "Mrs. Norton." It didn't matter, because we never knew these people; never met Mr. Graham or Mr. Jones or Mr. Norton. The food always came with a nice card wishing us well while our father was gone, signed with a flowery flourish by the Missus. And then one day Dad would be home, and he'd have presents for all of us: roses for Mom, clothes or music for Gina, toys or books for me.

When I was old enough to care, or old enough to realize that none of this was normal, I finally asked him why he always had to leave, why Gina and I were admonished not to keep secrets when it seemed like his entire life was a secret. I was twelve, two years before Gina would die.

"You can't ask me that," Dad said.

"It doesn't make any sense," I said.

"Scott," he said, "do you trust me?"

"Yes."

"Then know that I don't lie to you. I don't keep secrets. I omit. That's all. I just don't tell you things you don't need to know." My father looked pained, as if this conversation was one he'd already had, or had planned to have, but that none of it was working out quite as he remembered or anticipated. "You and Gina are not at risk. That's what you need to comprehend. Your mother is not at risk."

"I don't understand," I said.

"We choose the life we choose, Scott, and you live and you die inside of it. That's all I know to say. I don't think life would be easier for us if I worked at the Union 76 pumping gas. Maybe you'll understand that one day."

Gina stepped into the room then, and Dad asked her to sit down on the sofa with us. I remember the day as being near the holidays, around Christmas, and that there was a fire burning, and the house smelled of cinnamon and wrapping paper and bowls of baked Chex Mix, but the truth is that it could have been anytime, that it might just as well have been a Tuesday in September or March, one of those lost months when time seems in between action.

"Do you have concerns about my job, Gina?"

Gina shrugged. "It's your life."

"Right," Dad said, as if he were trying to convince himself that whatever she was saying was what he believed. "Well, I want you and Scott to know that eventually I'll be able to tell you everything. Almost everything. What I can tell you, I'm trying to say.

When you're eighteen or twenty-one or thirty or whenever it's right, we'll sit down and just hash it out so that you don't spend your whole adult lives mad at me. I don't want that."

I can see Gina clearly in my mind, and I can see my father, and I hear the words he said, and I can make sense of all of it; except that now, today, I don't know if it even happened like this at all. I think maybe Gina sat down between us and we watched TV in silence until Dad got up, went to the bathroom, and didn't come back out. Because that happened, too. Perhaps all that happened was my father told me what he told me and then, when Gina arrived, it all just stopped in place and I filled in the rest, added a final episode to the program.

Long before Gina died, and before that conversation with my father, I'd become obsessed with the great myths of our time: reincarnation, Bigfoot, UFOs, telekinesis, astral projection, and poltergeists. I was certain that my life had occurred at some point before I was born, that aspects of my world were too familiar, too much like a TV show I'd already seen and, when appropriate, I'd add moments from my memory to events, re-ordering their outcomes as I imagined they first were. Reliving them according to the patterns I thought I saw.

I'd sit in the library surrounded by books like *Twenty Cases Suggestive of Reincarnation*, ordering the symptoms of reincarnation, cataloguing the evidence, combing through the pages looking for mentions of dreams I'd had, or déjà vu experiences, hoping to find that I, like Suka, daughter of Sri Sen Gupta of West Bengal, had once been a woman named Mana and had, like Mana, tragically died of malaria in 1948. Or I'd imagine that I was Hans Holzer and that I could find all the ghosts of Great Britain, that I could unlock the true story of *Amityville Horror*, could meet and know people who knew who I was, who I was going to be, who I'd been.

Once, when Dad left on business for a week, I checked out all the books the Contra Costa Library had on the subject of past life regression—six—and spent the next several days reading them, until my mother finally picked up one called *Were You Joan of Arc?* and began flipping through it.

"You shouldn't read this," she said. "You'll have nightmares."

"I've read a hundred books just like it," I said.

"Still," Mom said. She was a young woman then—only in her late thirties—and I remember that she stood there and stared at me for a long time, not saying anything, the book under one arm.

"It's okay," I said eventually. "I don't think I was Joan of Arc."

"No," Mom said, "I can't see why you would. I just don't understand why you read these things. Why you need to learn about this when you could be learning about space or about science or about dinosaurs or anything, really."

"Because," I said, "I believe I've lived before."

Things exist beyond science and nature; I knew that then, and I *believe* that now.

My need for this reality is easily identifiable—a trained psychologist or even a talk show host with an above-average grasp of human nature could pinpoint the subtext of my life. I understand that I was predisposed to see things, to believe in things, to witness the cresting back of the Loch Ness monster on the day we set my sister back out into the world. Words in a book cannot alter true perception, I understand that. Even still, it is hard for me to say what I know is true: you don't choose the life you live and die in; you choose only to survive.

My mother and I sat on a wrought iron bench while Dad walked circles around the gravel-filled parking lot, weaving around tour buses and RVs, his hands buried deep in his pockets, his head down against the wind.

I always thought my father was a tall man, but as I grew older I found he was simply average in height, no different from me, or anyone, really. But he carried himself with a rigid poise, like an old prize fighter still caught in his stance. He had a presence, a solidity in build and stature that suggested power, and perhaps that is what I perceived. On that day in Scotland, however, he seemed diminutive to me, lost in scale around the enormity of the land-scape and the depth of sorrow I'm certain he felt. Whenever I see him now, no matter how happy he appears, part of him still looks like that man in the parking lot, a man I would never recognize as my own father had I not known it was him.

"It's not his fault," my mother said, watching her husband shrink against the weather. "He's a good person, Scott, I hope you know that."

"I want to," I said.

My mother wrapped one arm over my shoulder and squeezed me against her body. "You're not old enough to appreciate this," she said, "but he's sacrificed a great deal for all of us. Gina, too. He's a good person. He is." She shook her head once, slowly, and then pinched at her forehead. "Do you have a favorite memory of your sister?" she asked.

"No," I said.

"You must."

I tried to conjure in my mind a memorized detail that could stand for all the years I'd known Gina: the smell of her hair or the way she held the telephone; a hint of something familiar, a shared piece of us, a kind of filament. What I discovered was that she was already lost to me, that I remembered photos in albums, stories even, but that specific moments had vanished from my mind. I could not invoke her. All that I could see in my mind was the light beneath her bedroom door, the way it cast a yellow glow into my room every night at bedtime. It occurred to me then that I would never see that light again. How would I ever sleep?

"I didn't know I'd have to."

"It will come," Mom said. "You won't know when, but it will. I promise you."

Dad crossed the parking lot and made his way back toward us then, and I wondered how much he'd forgotten, how much expe-rience had become opaque in his memory. Every moment with my sister, every moment in my life up until that second, every action and reaction, had already faded into echo. I couldn't touch it, couldn't smell it, couldn't reason with the outcomes.

We waited for another hour, until most of the tourists were either on the water or eating lunch inside the small pub off the shore-line, and then made our way back to the water's edge with Gina's ashes. Dad had divided Gina into three separate bags so that each of us could dispose of her ashes in the way we saw fit; so none of us would be able to look back on this moment with regret, so that our choices were ours, our memories of the moment singular.

I'd like to say that became the case. I'd like to say that I've lived from this moment on without regret, but what makes a life worth living are the small calamities and the train wrecks we live through; a scar becomes a story of endurance.

Dad went first. He knelt down and dug a hole in the ground with his hands, tossing sand aside into a careful pile. When he was satisfied with the depth, he dumped his bag into the depression, took a deep breath, reached around the back of his head and yanked a clump of his own hair out from above his neckline. He drizzled the hair into the hole and then covered all of it again with the sand, tamping it down until it was smooth and fine.

"Jeff," my mother said quietly, "you're bleeding."

"I didn't want her to be alone," Dad said.

Mom kissed Dad lightly on the lips then, not in a romantic way or even in a sad way, but in a way I've come to recognize in both of them as a form of communication between two people who suffer the same pain, neither able to comfort the other. They divorced each other a few years ago. Not because they fell out of love, I don't think, but because each served the other as a constant reminder of what they'd lost, each seeing a part of Gina in the other.

They hugged for a moment longer, then Mom rolled up her pant legs and stepped into the shallows of the Loch up to her knees and stood unmoving in the frigid water, her back to us. She tilted her head toward the sky, and I could see that her lips were moving, but her words, if she said them aloud, were impossible to hear. In my memory, there is a glow around my mother, so that when she emptied her bag into the air and Gina spread out around her, the picture became hazy and distorted, already a dream even when it was happening. For a long time she stood just like that and cried, until Dad waded out beside her, not bothering to roll his pants up, and cried along with her.

Gina was their child. I understood that. I understood that a piece of both of them had disappeared and though I was behind them, holding Gina in my hands, their grief, their sadness, didn't have to include me.

I walked away from the shore, down past a rocky jetty and another dock filled with tourists awaiting a boat, and stopped finally beside a narrow bay. I could make out my parents in the distance still holding onto each other, their heads touching like lovers when really they were nothing more than tombstones marking a space. We have a death sentence that hangs over us, true enough, but in my life without my sister I've learned that death comes quickly, but that dying takes an eternity. She was only sixteen; I keep reminding myself of that. Maybe one day it will become an excuse and not merely a plea.

Gina's ashes poked through the small bag in odd angles. The myth of ashes is that they will be smooth, like spent briquettes, and that you won't see anything that seems organic. In truth, ashes are thick with fragments: tiny shards of bone, fine white slivers that could be a finger, an elbow, even a fingernail.

It can drive you crazy if you let it.

A body is not a person any more than a photograph of a monster is proof that it exists. Even still, as I felt Gina prodding my hand, tickling my palm, I knew she was still about, that she would haunt this place in my mind; that my parents, despite their secrets, despite the wedge that would grow between them, would likewise be visited by this day as if it were Gina's final on Earth. She killed herself for no particular reason we'd ever know—she was just sixteen!—and for that I welcomed the ghost.

And so, as I released her ashes into the water and watched as she rippled outward, I was not surprised to see a black form rise from the depths, beaded water refracting brilliant colors from the sun along its serpentine back and up over its neck and head. It whipped its forked tail from side to side, blinked its yellow eye, flipped over once, and was gone.

LOVE SOMEBODY

I did my cards the night before I picked Jasper up from McCallister. They said that shit was gonna really start piling up on us. Jasper got sent up for eighteen years, and did ten, after he'd gotten into a fight with Damon Selzer over how to operate a Slushie machine.

The fight happened at Sosa's Liquor Mart ten years ago because Jasper just had to have a root beer Slushie or he was gonna bust open. I was in the back looking at one of those magazines with the Polaroid beaver shots in them when I heard Jasper start to curse. I looked up in time to see Jasper turn the Slushie machine over on Damon's head and then start kicking him all over the place. Damon had Slushie oozing all over himself and looked like he was in a whole lot of pain.

Jasper really should of spent life in prison, considering he broke Damon's neck, but he and Damon are cousins. He plea bargained down to aggravated assault. In some places, family is still family.

I picked Jasper up in front of the prison, and I think the only other time I'd seen him look so happy was when he won first prize in the carrot competition in 4-H. He had a carrot that must have weighed five pounds. He said every time he had to piss he went outside and let it go on his carrot patch. He didn't tell that to the judges, of course, but I never ate any vegetables from his patch ever again. The prison gave him a corduroy suit that was too tight on the shoulders and too long in the leg. He looked like a circus clown, but I wasn't about to tell him that.

"How you been, Owen?" he asked me when he got into my car. He had a pinch of Red Man between his lip and teeth. He took off his jacket and tossed it into the back. His arms were covered with some splotchy tattoos.

"All right, I guess."

"Why the hell you still driving this Nova?"

I had a green Chevy Nova. I replaced the leather seats with some leopard skin ones because the leather gets so damn hot in the summer you can't hardly sit. It had a twin cam engine and some bad looking spoilers on it too.

"It's a sweet car," I said. "I ain't ever getting rid of it."

Jasper spit some chaw onto the floor. "We'll get some money in our pockets and get a coupla Caddies. How would that suit you?"

I thought about it for a minute. That would be fine, real fine. Even after being stuck away, Jasper still knew how to perk my interest.

When I woke up that next morning, things still didn't seem right. I checked my horoscope to see if my stars knew something I didn't, but everything seemed to be okay. Wasn't a full moon due for another two weeks. But I knew we were cursed as soon as Jasper told me he fucked his sister. He said, "It ain't like I broke a mirror." And I said, "You're right, you dumb son of a bitch. You should be on your knees praying you only get seven years bad luck." Jasper didn't care much about luck or curses or any of that stuff, but I did, and this wasn't something I could fix.

"It ain't like I raped her," Jasper said. "Besides, she's just a step. That isn't even illegal. Least I don't think." We were driving on Highway 35 just outside of Stillwater. You could see those little silvery mirages hanging on the road, and dust was kicking up swirls on the shoulder. I was glad I had the leopard seats because I was sweating through my jeans.

"Jasper," I said, "I don't even wanna know."

Jasper reached into his breast pocket and pulled out a flask of whisky and took a quick pull. He wiped his lips with the back of his hand and smiled. "You know what, I been thinkin' about it since I was in prison day one. I decided when I got out I was gonna start things off in a new direction." Jasper stopped and punched me hard on the arm, laughing. "You'd have done Molly, too, if you were in the same damn place as me."

"At the least you should've checked your stars before you did something this stupid," I said. "You would've seen the ramifications."

Jasper laughed and took another sip from his flask. "Hell, Owen, if I'd had sense enough to check my stars, do you think I'd of done it in the first place?"

I didn't answer him because for the first time I can remember Jasper made perfect sense to me. Jasper and me have a lot of history together—we been friends since the first day of kindergarten. He was playing up on top of the monkey bars, and I started climbing up one side, and he came over and kicked me in the face and told me to find some other place to play. My nose was broken pretty good and was really bleeding, so Ms. Wheaton made Jasper bite soap to teach him a lesson. She said he should know better because he'd been in the class last year and knew the rules about sharing. He told me he was gonna kill me for telling on him, but Ms. Wheaton told him that if he killed me he probably would never make it to first grade and that he should make friends with me while he still had the chance.

Since then we been pretty much inseparable. Well, of course, there was the ten years he spent in jail, but I tried my best to get in there with him. I must've robbed the same 7-Eleven in Tulsa five times and still never got caught. I never killed nobody because I don't wanna go to Hell. Now I know robbing people ain't exactly holy, but I think God is willing to overlook some of those things Moses talked about, except for killing. You know because He seen His share of that and probably still has a bad taste in His mouth about it. I don't mess with God.

We were driving to Oklahoma City so Jasper could visit his brother Norris who had his own congregation in the south borough.

It was a crappy part of town, and I wasn't real comfortable about taking my Nova there, but Jasper wanted to see Norris. Also, he'd heard about a Dairy Queen that was pretty easy to knock over. I figured what the hell; it was hot anyway and I love them dip cones. But now everything was in flux.

"You gonna tell Norris about Molly?" I asked. "It's the only way you can help this situation."

"Yeah, I'm gonna tell him that I fucked Molly and ask for God's forgiveness so we can rip off the Dairy Queen with the Lord behind us," Jasper said and then shook his head. "Good thing I went to the joint and not you 'cuz right now you'd be someone's little astrology-reading girlfriend. I swear to you Owen that you take this Dionne Warwick shit a step too far. Anyway," he paused for a moment and closed his eyes. I saw him mouth some words to himself while counting his fingers. "Yep, I'm right on this. What I done ain't even one of those Ten Commandments."

"I'm sure incest would've been on there," I said, "but nobody was sick enough in the head to think of it."

Jasper didn't respond, but I'm pretty sure he got the point. In another twenty-five minutes we would be in Oklahoma City. I went to school there at Oklahoma City Community College for about two years before they kicked me out for stealing a Xerox machine out of the library and then trying to sell it back to the school. They said it was either get the boot or go to jail so I opted for the boot. I don't have any hard feelings because I went back two years later and stole it again.

Norris's church was about a mile off the freeway in a neighborhood that was mostly black. I ain't got nothing against blacks, but Jasper about shivered every time he saw one. I didn't ask him what was up but figured it was a prison thing. Now, Jasper never wore a white sheet or burned crosses or anything, but he wasn't exactly voting for Al Sharpton either.

"Turn left up here," Jasper said. There was big white spire perched up above a little tree line in the distance. Jasper's brother

Norris is about seven years older than us and he's one of the holiest people I know. I remember when we were at Jasper's trial and Norris was on the stand as a character witness (mostly on account of he's the only guy who knew Jasper that didn't have any bench warrants in the county). The public defender asked him, "Can you tell the Court about your brother?"

Well, Norris looked across the room, and I swear it was like the Lord Himself told us to be quiet. Then he started a sermon about Jasper that made me think God had *two* sons. He went on for almost twenty minutes. Sure the DA, Kimble Treadway, objected a few times, but he didn't wanna cross Norris. I bet Kimble figured if anyone in the courtroom had some say about his distant future, it would be a preacher.

Anyway, I remember right at the end of his speech, Norris got up to a real pitch and said, "Now all of you people understand that Jasper is no worse than me, no worse than you, no worse than his cousin Damon—assuming he gets that full range of motion back, of course—and deserves to be treated fairly in this court. As in Genesis, chapter 31, verse 49, my brother Jasper needs to be looked over when he is apart from the Lord: 'And he said Mizpah, may the Lord watch over me and thee when we are absent one from another.' My brother has strayed, there is no doubt, but at heart he is a decent and caring man. A man of the Lord."

Well, Norris is quite a speaker, and everyone was thrilled by his sermon from the witness stand, but not a soul believed a word of it. I about chuckled a few times myself.

I parked my car next to the church van figuring no one would mess with it in such close proximity to the holy chariot. When we got out of the car I pulled my shirt off because it was some sticky weather and I was about to boil over. Jasper looked at me like I was crazy. "You can't go into my brother's church with all that hair on your back. Put a damn shirt on," he said.

"What do I care?" I said. "I'm just gonna keep my distance and wait for the lightning bolts to start raining down on you." Jasper gave me one of those looks that meant he was about to do something that involved battery, so I put my shirt back on. Norris's church was painted white and had a glittery facade above a set of double doors out front. I saw some kids playing basketball around the back side on a court that looked uneven and buckled.

"If we get a big haul from Dairy Queen," I said, "we should pay to have that court back there repaved. Bet kids turn their ankles on it all the time. It would be some good karma for both of us."

Jasper shrugged. "Norris won't take any money from me."

That was true. Much as Norris defended Jasper, he knew he couldn't save him.

We pushed the double doors open, and a wave of cool air brushed past us. The church was wide inside with six rows of pews and a big stained glass window. Jesus was up in the window and He had all kinds of colors hanging on Him. When Jasper and me were kids, our church had a Jesus that was about ten feet tall. Every time I went to church I swore He was looking right at me. Couple of times I thought He caught me picking my nose and rubbing snot on my Bible. He had these big sad eyes that I thought could blow a hole right through the back of my head. Norris's Jesus was smiling. No, that's not right. He was grinning. Grinning like He knew something that everyone else was just about to find out about.

Norris was sitting behind a small piano staring at a music book. He looked up at us and made a face somewhere between a frown and smile. "Do my eyes deceive me? Do I see a vision? Have the Philistines come unto Oklahoma City?" He started to laugh and then his fingers flew over the keys and the theme from *Jaws* echoed through the church. Norris stood up from the piano then and met us halfway across the church. I hadn't seen him since he married Ginny and me in '91 and I hardly recognized him. He was starting to get gray up around his sideburns and it looked like he was about five months pregnant. A peppery beard covered his face and a good part of his throat. But his voice gave him away. It was deep and husky sounding.

Jasper went right up and hugged him. I stayed a few steps behind and watched them. There was nothing hard about Norris, nothing that made you want to be afraid of him. After a couple of minutes, Norris pulled himself away and patted Jasper on the back. "When did you get out?"

"Couple days ago."

"You see Molly yet?" Norris asked. I couldn't stop myself from giggling. Jasper gave me his homicide look again, and I zipped it up.

"Sure did," Jasper said.

Norris sat down at the front pew and we followed him. "What do you think of my church?" he asked and swept his arms like he was the Shepherd, not the pastor.

"Helluva a lot nicer than the one at McCallister," Jasper said.

"You spend much time there repenting?"

Jasper shook his head and smiled. "Naw, but it wasn't a bad place to sit and think about ways to escape. Plus, they had the nicest toilet in the whole fucking place. Pastor kept that shit clean 'cuz all the families would come there after the executions. People thought they could catch their son's souls or something for a few last words." Jasper wasn't smiling now; he was just sort of staring at his feet and drooping his head. "Stupid people," he said.

Norris gave a look at Jasper and then put his hand on Jasper's knee and gave it a squeeze. "What about you, Owen, you been going to church with your wife?"

"Uh, no, I haven't," I said. "Not with her, I mean. She left me about three months after that wedding you did for me. Said I was too stupid to have a wife. She's probably right. But I been going off and on. Saying the Lord's Prayer and all that."

"You still a thief?"

Now, see, I ain't ever considered myself a thief. I've had a lot of honest jobs, just none as prosperous as taking stuff. A thief, that's a violent person in my opinion. Someone who'll knock you over and take your boots or something.

"Pretty much," I said. Norris doesn't care about definitions, so I just gave him an answer.

"You know," Norris said, "Jasper could probably go back to jail for just talking to you."

"I ain't ever going back to jail," Jasper said before I could answer. He was looking at Norris like he expected him to come back with something. But Norris just nodded.

Norris asked us to stay and watch his evening sermon, which was okay with us because we planned on going to Dairy Queen after dinner anyway. We sat in the back and watched the people assemble. They were mostly black, and I could see Jasper was getting all fidgety.

"What the hell's wrong with you?" I asked.

Jasper spit some chaw onto the floor, which I believe is not the kind of thing you want to do when you've already screwed with your luck, and looked over the room. "I just can't stand 'em," he said. "McCallister niggers rather fuck you than talk to you and that's the honest truth."

"Christ, Jasper, shut up," I said. "Norris hear you say that and he'll send you to Hell himself."

"Owen, you never understood. I can't give a shit about this. Not about God, Jesus, your damn stars, nothing. I ain't no college boy like you. I did time while you was drinking beer and fucking coeds. I was getting bitched around and no fucking Spirit was helping me out." Jasper was starting to get loud, and people were turning their heads to hear. Norris was up front talking to an elderly lady who was almost bald, and I saw him raise his head and look our direction. Jasper noticed and lowered his voice. "I'm trying to change. It ain't easy. You don't know what it's like."

I'd been in jail before but never the pen. Jasper had been pretty much beating ass since he was born and had himself a record of violent crimes. If he got picked up for something else, no matter what it was, he was gonna spend the rest of his life in prison. I didn't visit him much when he was in because I figured once I got there, folks probably keep me there. Jasper liked getting mail, so I wrote once a week telling him about what was going on in town, shit like that. Sometimes I'd send him the "Letters" part of *Penthouse* because he could usually sell it for something he wanted. I never asked him—not then, not later—what kind of shit went down in jail, because a man doesn't wanna talk about that. All he ever told me was that you gotta pay your dues, just like on the outside.

The congregation took their seats. Norris walked up to the pulpit and began sifting through some papers. Jasper was just staring out over the people with a quiet, dazed look in his eyes. Norris cleared his throat and began talking.

"I want to welcome you all here this evening," he said. "I'm proud to say that the Lord has blessed me with the presence of my own brother in my church. He is amongst you taking in God's word for the first time in a long time, and I'm extremely happy. Brotherhood. That is a very important topic that the Bible touches on and that we encounter every day. Helping each other, lending a hand when one of our friends is in need. But brotherhood comes in many forms. Blood does not mean brotherhood. Think, of course, of Cain and Abel. Cain looks God in the eye and says 'Am I my brother's keeper?' Took guts, but then he had just killed his own flesh. We must be willing to grab our brother's hands, touch them as God has touched us, and say 'Yes, I am my brother's keeper.' We must care for our people. No matter the color, the sex, the belief. We are all God's children."

I stood up and started clapping. Most of the people turned around and looked at me like I was some kind of fool, but damn if Norris didn't make everything sound so easy. I'd read in my Castaneda books that sometimes moments of absolute clarity can happen in the most unlikely of settings, and I believed I was having one of those. To myself I said, This is it. After today, no more stealing. No more fighting. No more nothing. I'm gonna get a job in

Stillwater, or maybe Tulsa, and get honest. Today is the last job. But I'd said that all before, to Ginny, and none of it happened.

Norris went on with his preaching, and I just kept listening. Jasper got up about halfway through his brother's sermon and smoked a cigarette outside. He was out there pacing in front of the Nova and kicking up rocks. When he came back in, his eyes were all runny.

"You okay?" I asked.

"Yeah, it's just all the damn dust. Ain't used to it anymore."

I knew he was lying. He knew he was lying. But we're like brothers, so it doesn't matter anyway.

After Norris finished his sermon, Jasper asked me to wait outside so he could talk to his brother in private. I was sitting on the hood of my Nova when an elderly man walked up to me and extended his hand.

"Your brother is a damn fine preacher, son," said the man. "A good Baptist." He was black and had gray hair edging up through the kinks in his head.

"I wish I could take credit for him," I said, "but he ain't my brother. Just an old friend."

The man shook his head. "You mean that trash he's talking to is his brother? That boy's looking like he spent some time in lockdown with those tattoos living up his arm. You look straight, though." He was squinting up at me, and I felt something start to turn in my stomach. "You're blue collar like the rest of us. Maybe a roughneck?"

"Naw." I just looked at the man. No matter how much Norris had said, this old guy didn't listen. "Naw, I'm a thief. Steal shit from people. Beat a lot of black ass when I can, sorta like a hobby. Feeling kinda edgy right now, in fact."

The old man shook his head and grinned at me like he'd had conversations just like this a thousand times over and each time, he'd come out standing. "Son, you ain't no thief. You hardly even a man." He stepped closer to me and put his finger on my chest. He was still grinning. "Twenty-third Psalm. You know it?" I shook my head. "'Thou preparest a table for me in the presence of mine enemies.' Your kind don't scare me anymore. I'm too old. But your friend, he got his own judgment." The old man stood there, his finger turning tight circles on my chest. "Best listen to Norris. Don't end up like Abel."

I watched the old man walk down the street, his right leg dragging a little bit behind him. He climbed into an old Buick Park Avenue and turned on the headlights. I stood up and waved, and he stuck his hand out of the window and waved back.

"Why the hell you waving to that poor son of a bitch?"

I turned around and Jasper was standing behind me. "Because he paid me a compliment. We had a conversation, something you should consider doing every once in a while with someone who ain't white."

"The hell's gotten into you, Owen? When did you become so fucking holy? You're a fucking petty thief, ain't even good enough to go to the pen. You can hardly piss straight without thinking twice about it and then checking your stars to see if you should hold it."

Jasper was right in my face, looking like he was ready to hit me. I ain't ever got into a tussle with him since that first day of school, and I wasn't about to start. But I stood my ground. "You don't know me anymore," I said. "I'm different than ten years ago. You know, I got some education. I learned about stuff and about people and I ain't no petty thief. I've been making a good living without you. I don't need you being Butch Cassidy anymore, because I'm doing just fine being Cly—" I stopped myself.

Jasper, who was scowling at me, started to twitch by his lips. He wanted to laugh. Hell, I wanted to damn near cry. "You mean," he said, "you're doing fine just being the Sundance Kid. Or—and I hope this ain't what you're saying—I'm Bonnie and you're Clyde."

"I meant you were Bonnie."

We both glared at each other, and then I couldn't hold it and started pounding my head with my hands because I was laughing so damn hard. Jasper sat down on the hood of the car and pulled the whisky flask from his pocket again. He turned it upside down in his mouth and then tossed it onto the dirt.

"I didn't tell Norris about Molly," he said. "Figured why kill the man, you know? But I told him I was gonna turn over the Dairy Queen. Just in case, you know, the whole parish was planning on getting dip cones together I didn't want some incident. But, uh, I told him you wasn't coming along. And that's the truth."

Jasper wasn't looking at me. He was rolling down his sleeves, covering up a tattoo of a mad looking clown on his forearm. "You got some education," he said. "You're right about that. I didn't. I just need one big haul, and then I can get out. Move to California, become a movie star or something."

I sat down next to Jasper. He got them eyes that say *don't fuck with me* and sometimes he got some eyes that say *everybody's fucked with me*. He was wearing the latter.

"Jasper," I said, "you know sometimes Norris would say shit to us when we were goofing off in Sunday school?" He nodded yes. "Well, I think about that sometimes. He would say that we were gonna go to Hell because we were taking money from the plate and peeping on the choirgirls. Shit, we done a lot worse since then. There's no place worse than Hell, but I believe God gotta put us somewhere."

Jasper sniffed a little and wiped his eyes. "Hell don't mean shit, Owen. Ten years I've been up in that sty, and it's been a daily trough of piss: tortured, fucked, everything. Don't mean shit. You know why?"

"We don't have to talk about this," I said. "You got your life and I got mine now. How it shakes out, Jasper, that don't depend on us. Those decisions were already made."

"You know, if I hadn't broke Damon's neck," Jasper said, "I might've broke yours or Molly's or, shit, you know? Someone's. But that time away, man, I learned to imagine shit that is much more important than your God or your Oujia board crap. I read books about philosophy, law, all kinds of shit. You know, I even got my high school diploma. But I also found out, that ain't me. I'm a crook. Always been. And that's the fucking deal."

Two little girls in dresses walked hand-in-hand out of the church, their arms swinging back and forth while they sang a song about Jesus. They couldn't have been more than six years old, and both of them were pretty in that way where you can tell they're gonna be someone's problem come about sixteen. But for now, their world was as big as it would ever need to be, and I'm not shy to admit I envied them. So much time. So many choices to make.

"You ever wish you were that old again? Start this shit all over again?" I asked.

"Fuck no," Jasper said. "Norris, he made the right moves, you know? But I wouldn't want that life. He just told me that he didn't wanna ever see me in his church again 'cuz I had the look of the devil in me. He said he lied for me once, but never again. Maybe he's right, you know? Maybe I'm a piece of shit. But I'll be damned if I'm gonna die poor."

I leaned back against the windshield and stared up at the stars. If you're away from the city lights, ain't no place better in the world to see stars than Oklahoma. Only class I ever failed at the community college was astronomy, 'cuz the damn teacher and I got in an argument about astrology.

Jasper craned his neck back and faced the sky. "You'd die in prison. You don't ever see no damn stars." I sat back up and put my hands up over my eyes and squeezed. I had so much going on in my head. So many thoughts and little pictures of things I fucked up on, I wanted to see if I could pinch real hard and get them to shoot out my ears.

I'd been in love with Ginny for a long time, married her, tried to have me a kid every night for three months, and then got caught buying a hooker in Tulsa. I'm so dumb. Ginny hooked me up straight, working at Eskimo Joe's at the bar. I was making good money. We were happy as shit. I told her, "No matter what happens, I ain't ever gonna lose you." She said, "When Jasper gets out of jail, he ain't welcome in our home." I said, "Fine." She was smart enough to know what trouble was; I wasn't smart enough to realize it was me.

"I ain't doing this anymore," I said.

It was still and muggy outside and I felt sticky all over. My momma used to say that on quiet summer nights, if you listened real hard, you could hear God breathing. All I heard was Jasper, and he was crying. I didn't say anything to him; I just put my arm over his shoulder and gave him a kind of hug, the only one I had ever given a man.

We sat there in front of Norris's church for about an hour, until Norris poked his head out the door, smiled faintly, and locked it. I gave Jasper the keys to my Nova and told him I would report it stolen in about two hours. He said that would be fine. He said that he'd get a new car at the Dairy Queen, something a little less noticeable on the road. A Caddie or something, he said.

I shook his hand and told him to have good luck, that even though he fucked his sister, at least he'd come to peace with himself. Jasper pulled me toward him and hugged me hard. I could smell old whisky and sweat, and I felt his beard press against my cheek. Then he did something I'll never forget: he kissed me, his lips catching half of mine. Then he just turned around, got into my Nova, and left.

Jasper got the Dairy Queen for a load of money. Robbed every damn person in it, and the store. On the news, they called it an "Old West reign of terror," but ain't nobody got shot or hurt or nothing, just robbed. I like to think Jasper made it to California and is riding around town in a fat old Caddie with some actress by his side. They're just smoking cigars and living it up.

I walked home that night along Highway 35 and thought about all kinds of shit that I'd done. Talked to myself a little, like some kinda crazy man would, and even told myself some jokes. The night was full of noises: crickets, frogs, and stuff that sounds like it might kill you. I stopped once to smoke a cigarette. I lit a few matches and tried to read the lines in my palm but the night was too dark. About five cop cars flew past me, sirens blaring.

DISAPPEAR ME

I'm in a sex shop in San Francisco watching my father buy a leather jumpsuit for his gay lover. It is my father's lover's birthday today; I know this because my father has also just stopped by the Hallmark store and purchased one of those funny greeting cards with a naked man inside.

My father has aged well. I'm standing closer to him than I usually do, so I take time to really look at his face. I study the hard line of his jaw, the fine plastic surgery that has sucked away the heavy wrinkles around his eyes. Dad is good looking.

Dad steps up to the cashier and purchases the jumpsuit. There is a smile on his face. The cashier offers him a courtesy gift-wrap, but Dad says he'll just eat it as he walks. They both laugh. He steps quickly toward the door and I nearly stumble over a stack of porn movies stacked on the floor.

Dad walks out of the store and directly into a woman dressed in a smart business suit with her hair piled high on top of her head. "Carl, what in the world were you doing in there?" she says to my dad.

"Oh, a friend of mine is getting married," Dad says. "You know, something zany for the bachelor party."

The woman laughs in a way I have come to find familiar since I disappeared. She knows my dad isn't going to some bachelor party where a leather jumpsuit with not-so-conspicuous zippers would be appropriate. She also knows my dad has some bigger issues. She's no dummy, whoever she is. I mean, everyone gets those flyers in the mail with my picture on them, and my brother's Scout troop still hands out leaflets in front of Safeway. Thousands of teenagers go missing every year, but at least I am well publicized.

I follow Dad back to his car. He talks to himself a lot when he walks; not loudly like a transient might, something above a mumble. Today he is mad. "Just a bachelor party. Stupid answer. I don't care." Dad tosses his boyfriend's gift into the trunk and then looks up and down Polk Street for a long while. I wonder if maybe he is looking for me. "Pretty bird. Pretty bird," he says when a pigeon walks up to his feet. "I don't have anything for you," he says and keeps staring at the bird, like he is waiting for a response, and then he suddenly lunges forward, arms flailing. The pigeon skips back onto the curb where I am standing and struts between my legs and off toward the sewer.

My dad laughs in a way that isn't all that funny, then checks the street again before getting into his car and driving off. I don't follow him because I'm not a superhero or anything. I don't drive an invisible car or fly an invisible plane. I usually take public transportation.

There was a time when I thought this was all fantastic. That time has passed into something close to comfort. I've come to grips with my new identity and the people I meet now who share many of my fears, my dreams, my problems. We are a community of freaks maybe, but a community nonetheless.

"Tell me something," Lydia says to me. "Do I look like I've lost any weight?"

This is an old joke so I play along. "You do look a little thin," I say.

We are sitting on a bench across from Pac Bell Park. It is warm today and the breeze off the Bay feels like a cool drink. "You always say the right things, Billy," Lydia says. "Someone raised you smart."

Long lines of people are filing into the stadium to see the Giants play the Mets. "Ever been to New York?" I ask.

"A hundred times," Lydia sighs. "Before all of this I did quite a bit of traveling."

Lydia is a Human Trampoline. She is as thin as a grain of sand and well over ten feet tall. Though she is not invisible like me, she is nonetheless very difficult to perceive. But she can bounce. She took the TransAmerica Building in one hop. There were reports in some of the tabloids that she had been spotted, but it is next to impossible.

"You could jump the Empire State Building?" I say.

"In my sleep," she says.

"So why not give it a shot?"

Lydia kneels down so that we are almost at eye level. She is older than me by only a few years, though I can tell that she thinks of me like a son, especially when she kneels down so that I can really see her.

"What if I'm the only one there?" she says. "What if I get to New York and there's no one like us? It's just a bunch of those talking dogs and a couple of dolls that really do come to life after the kids go to sleep. I couldn't deal with that kind of rejection. Not now, I'm too far along."

I've been gone for over a year, but Lydia has made a career out of this. A bank of clouds floats above the stadium, and I make out the thin outline of Thomas the Cloudburster near the gray center. Lydia spots him, too, and waves her hand absently. "See, Billy, Thomas has it all," Lydia says. "He can just turn with the weather. He doesn't have to worry about where he would fit in. He is in his element."

My friend Wanda says that it's not about fitting into places, but I choose not to say anything to Lydia about that. The wind turns south, and Thomas is gone.

"I saw my Dad today," I say, hoping to change the subject, but I can tell by the way Lydia is looking at the Bay that she is ready to hop.

"Was he with that guy again?"

"No," I say, "not this time."

Lydia lifts a finger into the air to test the wind. "I think I can clear the stadium," she says. It's like this with her. Short attention span. And with a simple torque of her knees, she's off. A few children tilt their heads up, sure that they saw *something*, but by the time they have a chance to process the information, she's gone. I see her touch down across the peninsula and then she's airborne again, this time back toward Sausalito.

For a while I drift through the stadium listening to the people, sometimes stopping long enough to watch the game. The smell of the grass is so much stronger now in my new condition, and I think that the blades seem more pointed. Focus has become everything.

I could have used this focus during my last days of visibility. I'd found the address of the man my father was sleeping with in the phone book. He had mentioned him a dozen times in the last month for various reasons, and each time, my mom got this look on her face that made my little brother Jeff cry. "He's in Marketing," Dad said once. "A real comer," he said another time during dinner. "The kind of guy who makes the people around him work harder. You know what I mean, Joanie?" My mother got up from the table and came back with a bottle of wine. Once, a commercial came on for a new laptop computer and Dad said, "Oh, that's like the one the new guy in Marketing has," and Mom just got up off the couch, grabbed the car keys, and left for two days.

Dad kept talking about this guy in little ways. By the sixth or seventh time, I found myself getting up, like Mom, and locking myself in my bedroom. I would turn the stereo on as loud as I could until my ears were numb from the bass kick. *I want to be gone. I want to be gone. I want to be nowhere.*

So I went to his house. Dad's car was parked in the driveway. Nobody was around in the neighborhood so I climbed this big tree that hung over the back fence of the guy's yard. A window was open on the second floor of the house, and I could hear Dad's voice, every word. A row of venetian blinds blocked my view. I didn't need to see any more than I could hear.

But I had to.

I inched along the branch I was sitting on until I was so close to the window that I could have reached through and touched my father.

"You don't want to do that," a voice whispered to me. "You wanna climb down and go home," the voice said. "You don't need to see this."

But I stayed. I stayed and listened to the sounds of lovemaking. I listened to my Dad say the most tender things I could ever have imagined about his lover, about his children, about *me*, and even about his wife, my mom.

When my dad rose from the bed and got dressed in the expensive gray suit my mom had picked out for him at Macy's, he decided to open the venetian blinds. Dad decided just then that he needed a fresh breath of air. He needed to open those blinds and see his son between two large branches.

It all seems so avoidable now.

I meet Wanda in Union Square and we just walk for a while, not talking or even pretending to be careful about who we bump into. We do this sometimes, because, as Wanda says, it is good to be human every now and again. You forget what skin feels like, how there is warmth in even the slightest touch. You forget how to remember someone by their smell.

Wanda has been here from the start. She was the one who taught me the rules of the game. There aren't many things to remember, but they are all important. You can be heard, you can be felt, you can fall, you can injure yourself, you can cry, you can sing songs, you can mourn, and you can wrap yourself in all the gauze you want, but no one will ever see you. You can love the world, but you can never go back.

At first I was relieved to see the others: the Lydias, the Thomases. But it was Wanda who made me family. And it was Wanda who took me from that tree.

Wanda leads me down into a BART tunnel, and we hop on a

train bound for the East Bay. It is rush hour so all the seats are taken. This is how Wanda prefers it. We can talk out loud, and no one notices over the din of the train.

"What do you miss?" Wanda looks at me like she thinks I might lie to her, which I won't.

"I miss my Nana's and Popa Dave's basement," I say. "There were these great old recliners down there that smelled just like them, and old toys from when my dad was a kid."

"I miss calling my sister on the phone," Wanda says. "She was a big fat woman, you know, so I used to let the phone ring ten, fifteen times before I would hang up. That way if she didn't make it to the phone, at least she knew it was me."

We are under the Bay. The train is creating a loud humming sound that makes everything feel like it is vibrating. "I bet she felt better whenever you called," I say. "Even if she didn't get to talk to you."

"Maybe," Wanda says.

I thought for a long time that Wanda didn't exist, that she was just a memory from my childhood. She remembers the lean years, she tells me, when I'd pushed her into the back of my mind and refused to believe she was there. "Like the time you faked a cold so you could stay home and watch the baseball game," Wanda says. "And nearly set the house on fire in the process!"

And of course she was there with me in the tree. That voice I heard in my head was Wanda's. When my father opened the window and saw me, Wanda did the only thing she could do; what I'd been asking her to do for so long.

"I know what you're going through, Billy," Wanda says. The BART train stops in Fremont, and passengers file out around us. Wanda motions over to a pair of seats that have become empty, and we sit down. "You're starting to miss real life, aren't you?"

"No," I say. "I just want to make things right. Let my mom know that I'm not a Peruvian sex slave or something. Let her know that I'm okay."

"Your mom," Wanda says, "needs you."

"I know," I say.

"Just be subtle," she says.

Across from us, an old man sitting alone begins to cough violently. Wanda looks concerned. She gets up and sits down beside him, placing her mouth close to his ear. This is Wanda's gift. Her business of reassurance and support, she calls it. She says it's her place to make change in people. To comfort. "I expect to hurt valiantly," she says. I don't know how old Wanda is, and I've never asked. All I know is that she has hurt enough for all of us. That's why she's here.

Though I know I'm different, it all still hurts. That's what's so confusing. There is a dead end to my family now, a helplessness that makes my parents stay together despite all that is between them. Maybe they stay together for my brother, maybe for the memory of me. I believe, though, that there was always a border between my parents, even before I disappeared and before my father started having his affairs. I can clearly remember peering into my parents' room as a child and watching them cling to each other, their bodies moving in a direct rhythm. It seemed so deliberate—passionless, unforgiving, and without patience.

I am thinking this in my parents' house. It is a Tuesday, and I am standing in the family room, staring at my mom. She leans over the sink in the kitchen, her long brown hair pulled back away from her face. There is an absentness to my mother; her skin is pale and hard, her eyes flat. She looks like she is floating.

When I was a child, before my brother was born, Mom used to read me to sleep. She told me that all stories are someone else's dreams, that in stories anything can happen. There were curious monkeys, velveteen rabbits, wild things that lived in closets, and trees that gave and gave until they had nothing left to give.

There is a gulf between that time and now. And as I watch her scrub the broiler pan, I wonder if she even remembers it. She still has Jeff, my brother, and in some ways she continues to hang onto my father, though she knows he is gone also.

Mom turns from the sink and pulls a clean glass from a cabinet. She goes to the refrigerator and doesn't open it. She stares at a picture of me taken on a soccer field ten years ago.

"Billy," Mom says. My heart feels thin in my chest. I hear it making clicking noises.

My baseball trophies and soccer awards have all been removed from the den. The pool table is gone, replaced by a long, solid oak desk and a computer. Dad sits on the leather couch and reads the *San Francisco Examiner*. On the television, Tom Brokaw talks about the fleecing of America.

There are scratches down the back of Dad's neck.

Mom is at the desk searching the Internet for me. She looks for articles that mention my name, updated lists of missing or runaway children. There are chat rooms for families of missing children, and she reads other people's stories, though she never joins in to tell hers.

Dad has never told her that he saw me. Never told her that he opened the window on the second floor of his lover's house in Concord and saw me melt into thin air.

Never once has he said, "You know what, honey, I saw Billy evaporate." He knows I was there. There have been times when I've sat next to Dad in the front seat of his car and listened to him recount the scene to himself. "I saw you," he always says. "I saw you, Billy."

Jeff walks into the den and switches the channels on the TV. Dad starts to say something, stops.

"Time to go," Wanda whispers in my ear. I don't know how long she has been behind me.

I could just live here, invisible, taking part in the everyday life of my family. I could sleep in my bed, eat in my kitchen, and walk through the halls of my home. I could live like a phantom:

benevolent, occasionally playful. I could even be scary sometimes. I could follow Dad when he went out to see his lover, and this time I could change some things.

There are four walls that pluck at me here, make me want to give up what I've found outside this old life. There are blue skies and windows and picnics and everything else that never quite happened before.

Others have tried. There is Wilson who lives with his family in Cleveland. Lydia told me about him. He is a success story. But then there is Nancy who forgot she was still human, forgot that walls and mirrors hurt when you run into them. Forgot that her fragile little skull was still made of bone and skin and that what people could not see could still be damaged. Forgot that to die invisible is to really die alone, no matter if you are in your own home or in some fantastic castle in the south of France.

I watch Jeff from a distance. I sometimes follow him through the mall after school. He always stops in front of the Club Med Vacations kiosk and looks at brochures, his fingers running over the blue water and tanned bodies that dot the pages. At the Orange Julius he orders a foot-long hot dog and a strawberry smoothie, spreads out a five dollar bill on the counter and flattens it with his palm.

Jeff is usually alone. He doesn't talk to himself or make odd noises, but he does try to make eye contact with each person he sees. There is something disquieting in this, especially in the way most of the adults quickly stare down at their feet or busy their hands. He's only ten.

Though we are separated by nine years, an eternity for brothers, there has always been a connection between us. When Jeff was still just a fetus, I could sit for hours talking to my mother's belly, telling him stories, jokes, singing him my favorite songs.

With me gone, too much has descended on Jeff, and he can't handle it most of the time. Mom often forgets that Jeff is still *here*.

In her angriest moments, my mother tells Jeff he was a mistake, that my father wanted him aborted, but that she saved him. Too much for a ten-year-old to hear, Wanda says, too much for anyone to hear.

Jeff lies. To everyone. He tells his teachers at school that the police now believe I was abducted and forced to join an outer space cult like those people in San Diego. Not true. The police think I am a runaway. He tells his best friend, Luke Kastner, that the police believe I became a Muslim and am currently under investigation for several terrorist bombings. He is only a child, Wanda tells me, let him deal with things as a child would.

I should have never left my brother.

I stand behind him while he takes a math test involving complex fractions. He misses several easy questions because he is at that stage in his life where being dumb is considered cool.

Jeff and I are all we have anymore, but he doesn't know it. He's too old to have an invisible friend and too young to become like me. Meanwhile, he can only live his life within this family I escaped, for better or worse.

Ysrael pulls me aside one afternoon when he sees me window shopping near Pier 39. "Ah," he says. "It's the incredible invisible boy wonder!"

I smile and give him a little bow.

"You are in the paper today," he says.

I look at his feet, and there I am on the front page.

"I hear they have found your body," Ysrael says, laughing.

The paper says that the body of a teenage boy has been found in a shallow grave off a wooded hiking trail on Mt. Diablo. Though badly decomposed, police suspect the body belongs to me.

"Quite a twist of fate," Ysrael says.

There is a quote from my father. He says, "I hope we can finally put this to a close and get on living our lives in peace."

I find Wanda sitting in the front seat of an Aerostar double parked in front of Fisherman's Wharf. There are two small dogs and a child of maybe three sitting alone in the back seat. I show her the paper.

"I know," she says. "Saw it this morning." The child looks up at the sound of Wanda's voice and smiles.

"What do I do?"

"Let them believe," she says. "It's best for everyone."

"What about the family of the dead boy?" I ask.

"Don't worry," she says. "We've done this before."

So let's say my parents bury this boy and pretend it is me, and Wanda fixes it for his real family, and everyone has a little bit of closure. Let's imagine Mom and Dad make it right for each other again, and maybe Jeff finds a little peace in adolescence.

Maybe Mom and Dad don't make it right, but at least Dad tells Mom all the things he told his lover the day I disappeared. Things like how fun it was when they spoke in that goofy voice to each other, or how he didn't ever tell her the truth about his affairs because he couldn't bear to hurt her.

Maybe all these things happen, and the world starts spinning properly again. Do I stop visiting the house every other week? Do I stop following Jeff to the mall? Do I read my obituary over and over again until it becomes my definition of infinity? Do I slip into some kind of crazed depression where it feels like time is an illness? Or, when everything is right, will I just reappear?

Wanda tells me all of this is natural, a process of eliminating the tangible. Lydia, the Human Trampoline, tells me that I am growing every day. She tells me that there is a spark to me that she hasn't seen before. "You are here during a great time," Lydia says. "This is your history," she says, and then she is airborne, jumping high over the Golden Gate Bridge, the wind lifting her, making her soar.

"The only way you can help your family is to let them mourn," Wanda says, and then she takes my hand in hers and leads me to a park bench where we sit for a long time. The air around us is alive, and the sunset has a watery glory.

I know that I am a species of some kind of love. No matter the condition of that love now, I am a symptom of what used to be gentle kindness between two people. There is no body. There is no flesh.

But, there is purpose. I am here for a purpose. Wanda is, too. We all are. We aren't miracle makers or magicians. We only love your children when you won't.

RISE, JOHN WAYNE, AND REBUKE THEM

Ira looked out over the field of combatants, all fifteen hundred of them, and wondered when, exactly, he'd lost his mind. He figured it was probably 1997, but he couldn't be sure. Below him a group of young men wearing Greek letters across their chests were being outfitted with berets, swords, and, in some cases, flowing beards. It never failed to amaze Ira how fraternity boys, gang bangers, and militia types always wanted to be the Republican Guard. Ira figured it had something to do with mob mentality or the sense that they were the bad guys, the kind of people who tortured first, asked questions later. Perhaps that was a fun thing to be when most of the time life just happened to you, without any kind of power exertion. But didn't they realize that the Republican Guard always lost in these simulations?

It was definitely 1997, he decided. That was the year he bought up the twenty-six hundred acres surrounding the north shore of the Salton Sea—California's putrid, rank and polluted inland sea—under the false assumption that one day the state would clean the sucker up and he'd have the perfect spot for a resort hotel and golf course. Timeshares were an option. Perhaps a retail board-walk. Bumper cars. A Ferris wheel. A performing arts school. A Native American cultural center. It was all right there in front of him, presuming, naturally, the State did something about the smell. And really, he thought then, once you stood out there long enough, the stench of rotting fish, sewage run-off, and the sulfuric aroma of red tide did begin to abate some.

"I want a divorce," his wife Carol said the first time he brought her out to look at the land.

"Half of this is yours," Ira said.

"I want the portion that's underwater," she said.

Of course, he thought, 1998 wasn't exactly a marvel, either. Ira's decision to install coffee bars in each of his six local car washes had backfired in the most mundane way: more than half the people who visited HandyDandy Wash did so because they'd spilled something on their seats, usually coffee, usually that damn Starbucks coffee in those white cups that his staff constantly fished from beneath seats of SUVs and sedans alike; those white cups that filled his trash cans every afternoon and evening after the goddamned Starbucks moved in next door and began selling better coffee at more expensive prices, but without the attendant aroma of Windex and Turtle Wax.

It was business abortion, he thought. And maybe he shouldn't have borrowed the money from the Iranian guy, but whatever. You do what you do when you do it. And maybe he shouldn't have called immigration when he couldn't pay up. He regretted that. Sayid was a good man with a certain industrialized sense of ethics—and Ira appreciated that to an extent—the extent ending at threats of physical violence.

All of which brought Ira back to the Salton Sea. After Carol left him and Sayid got deported—threatening all the while to have him killed in a way that was painful and sexually humiliating—Ira figured the Salton Sea would be the absolute last place anyone—be they assassins or lawyers—would come looking for anyone. For a month he lived in a yurt and tried his best to commune with something, but the fact of the matter was that he couldn't find anything valid enough to place his trust in. God? Not results heavy. Nature? A fickle bitch. Acid? Made him too paranoid. X? Too sexually enticing, which, when alone, only led to chafing. Alcohol? All liquor ever did was make him cry for Carol and that was one thing he was able to accomplish without stimulation.

Carol.

He'd loved her, of course. They'd had fifteen good years together and in the end, when she walked out, it didn't feel like real life. No, he thought, it felt like a scene in a movie he'd rented once but had fallen asleep in the middle of, only to wake up during the last five minutes. He knew the basics, had a strong expectation of how things had likely occurred based on past history and motivations, but damn if he could accurately say what the story really was.

But now, as he stood on his observation deck and watched the people—men, women, teenagers, even a few toddlers—reenacting the first Gulf War, the numerous battles for the Gaza Strip and the ongoing guerrilla struggle for Iraq, it occurred to him that Carol did the right thing by walking out, though he guessed that she probably wished she'd waited long enough to cash in on WarTime.

"It smells like a corpse out here," she told Ira the day she came out to have him sign the divorce papers. They'd already been separated for more than a year.

"You get used to it," he said. He had two yurts then and had even managed to get DSL access from the Park Ranger's station.

"You never get used to something you hate," she said. "You think Sayid is used to living in Iran again? Even that's better than this shithole."

"What does it matter, Carol?"

"I just hate to see you like this," she said. "Out here like you're John Wayne fighting some war. It's silly."

Even as Carol droned on about their dog Skipper and a mutual fund they'd need to liquidate, Ira could see his future, could smell the stench of diesel fuel and sweat and the way he'd be able to turn his acres of skunk land into gold, into oil, into relevance. It did smell like a corpse, and that, Ira knew, was not a smell that was easy to replicate.

A guttural chant rose up from the young men beneath him, a pidgin Arabic that embarrassed Ira every time he heard it—not

because the chant was really ABBA's "Dancing Queen" phoneti-
cally translated and then photocopied onto 3x5 cards emblazoned
with the flag of Iraq (a personal joke Ira actually appreciated) but
because the people who did the chanting honestly believed they
were speaking to the same God their real-life Iraqi counterparts
had before literally falling on their swords.

If John Wayne were to materialize on one of the meticulous-
ly recreated Middle Eastern battlefields Ira had carved into the
landscape—replete with the burned-out hulls of oil tanker trucks,
Humvees, and decommissioned Soviet-era tanks he'd purchased
for a tidy sum—no one would even recognize him. Hell, Ira thought,
watching the fraternity boys marching out to battle, they'd probably cut the Duke's damn head off.

If there was one thing Ira Loomis didn't understand about human
nature, it was the need to feel pain in lieu of feeling nothing at
all. It was right there in the evening status report filed by his
Intelligence Advisors and faxed to his home in Rancho Mirage.
Each night, while he drank his one glass of good scotch and nibbled
on whatever take out food he'd picked up on his way in from the
Salton Sea, Ira pored ever the reports, noting issues he'd need to
bring up with his staff in the morning. It was usually nothing
major—a broken leg, an unexploded ordnance discovered in one
of the tanks, public drunkenness—and invariably the reports noted
that all was well on the Middle Eastern front, at least business-
wise, which pleased Ira. On the news, someone was always killing
someone else over there and that meant tour groups and right wing
Christian nutjobs out for a little Biblical vengeance would keep
booking time. But tonight, a report from sector five—where a faction
of Microsoft execs and a PTA from Merton, Wisconsin, were reenacting, by special request, Carter's failed attempt to free the
hostages from Iran, except that they'd paid extra for a little dream
fulfillment, including a full fledged attack on the embassy by the
American Special Forces—had Ira troubled: an isolated sniper attack

by a man not affiliated with either group, who appeared shirtless and covered in suntan lotion, screaming obscenities and firing non-lethal bean bag rounds.

It was the fifth time in two months that Ira's younger brother, Cliff, had shown up just to fuck with people and it was beginning to weigh on Ira. What was it in Cliff that mandated he be a constant pain in the ass? Why couldn't he just be happy?

Ira had hired his brother to be the VP of Group Sales and Corporate Event Planning after it became clear he couldn't get decent applicants to haul their asses out to the Salton Sea for a job, no matter how lucrative. For the first couple of months, Cliff was a charm. He'd beat Ira into the office by fifteen minutes, at least, every morning. If they needed someone to greet a private jet or helicopter out at the runway at dawn, Cliff would be there in a suit and tie with coffee and bagels. If Ira just wanted to drive into Los Angeles for the day, catch a movie, maybe get a massage and a facial, the full executive treatment package, Cliff assumed command of the ship and never once ran it into an iceberg.

Then, just as quickly, Cliff started asking for more. More responsibility. More of a profit-percentage stake. More say in research and development.

"You're a good people-person," Ira said to his brother, "but you're not a businessman. Why not just relax and do the easy stuff, make your money, and let me worry about all this other crap?"

Ira realized as he was telling his brother this that he sounded vaguely like Michael Corleone talking to his brother Fredo in *The Godfather II*. That wasn't such a bad business model, he thought, provided Cliff didn't try to have him murdered at some point.

"I think you're underestimating what I bring to the table," Cliff said. "Like Vietnam, you know? People would love to fight that shit again. Rambo and all that. We plant some trees out here by the water's edge and we got the South China Sea. Get away from this Holy War shit."

It was an idea, Ira acknowledged, but too much of the

company's tourist influx was Asian, and that just wouldn't appeal to them. No Japanese person would portray a Vietnamese or Cambodian; same with the Koreans and Chinese.

"Fine," Cliff said. "Then let's do the Bay of Pigs. You know how many people would come out to do the Bay of Pigs?"

The problem was Cliff just didn't see things in wider world view. No one gave a shit about Cuba anymore. Yeah, they got riled up about that Elian Gonzalez kid, but no one was going to pay the big bucks to fight for him. In the end, the whole conversation devolved into a series of personal attacks until Ira told Cliff to pack his shit up and go if he was so unhappy, and Cliff had done just that.

It was so stupid, Ira thought now, pouring himself his second scotch, because it was impossible to think Cliff was actually unhappy at the time. He earned a high six-figure income, was fucking Phyllis, his personal assistant, and got free use of any of the company Hummers. Shit, Ira was *still* paying him his salary, three months after the row. But this sniper business was unacceptable. Ira made a note to have Cliff apprehended and removed if this happened again. Maybe he'd call his mother in the morning, too, just for good measure.

Ira spent the rest of the evening sitting outside on his patio, watching the sprinklers water the thirteenth fairway of the golf course he lived on. He was fascinated by the cycle of the sprinklers, how a barren desert had been transformed by a few key inventions. It reminded him of his car wash business, a job he actually enjoyed until that whole coffee fiasco. Both the desert and the car wash were dependent on the same basic issue: water and the effective misuse of it. If he'd just been able to focus on the water, on keeping things clean and tidy, he wouldn't be sitting alone in a gorgeous house covered in the stink of his own invention.

When Ira got to his office at WarTime the next day, Carol was sitting in the foyer with Skipper, their golden retriever. Ira had custody of Skipper on alternating weekends, major holidays, and pretty much whenever he wanted the dog, which ended up being about six months out of the year when he factored in Carol's hectic traveling schedule now that she was married to Sayid. The truth was, Ira obsessed constantly about Skipper, reasoning that he'd made a commitment to the dog that wasn't as fungible as the one he'd made with Carol. There was a tacit agreement between man and dog that man wouldn't just up and leave if he became dissatisfied with some other non-dog portion of his life, and Ira felt a debt to that. Skipper was always fair to him, understood that sometimes a man has to rat another man out to survive, and felt, Ira believed, that Carol and Sayid did not love each other as much as Ira and Carol once had, but tolerated the situation nonetheless.

"Thanks for showing up on such short notice," Ira said.

"No, it's fine," Carol said.

"I was just feeling down last night," Ira said. "I shouldn't have called."

"I said it was fine, Ira."

"I know, I know," Ira said. Skipper slept on the floor at Carol's feet, his head flat across his front paws, his back left leg twitching slightly. Ira knelt down and patted the dog's back. "How's he doing?"

"He's fourteen," Carol said.

Ira nodded once. He tried to remember the first time he saw Skipper, the first time he'd looked into the dog's eyes and seen that thing that makes you fall in love with a beast, but all he could conjure in his mind was a picture he once took of Carol and Skipper asleep on the sofa together, a pack of their own. He hadn't seen the picture in years, but remembered it more than he remembered the experience itself.

"Why did we name him Skipper?"

"What?" Carol said.

"I can't recall why we named him Skipper. Isn't that weird? I should know that."

Carol stood up and brushed dog hair from her skirt. "I have to go," she said. "Sayid is waiting in the car and he gets very uncomfortable here."

"He shouldn't," Ira said.

"You had him deported and then built an amusement park where you kill him every day," Carol said.

"He should grow up," Ira said. "It's not always about him."

"I didn't come here to fight with you," Carol said. "You wanted to see Skipper and I brought him. Okay?"

"Okay," Ira said. He watched his ex-wife walk out of his office building (what he actually called Command Center Alpha in the literature that went out to prospective investors and Hollywood film crews) and into the bright sun of the desert morning. A black Mercedes with tinted windows pulled up to the curb. Carol opened the passenger door, paused, said something to Sayid, then turned and came walking back into the foyer.

"Technically," she said, "his name isn't Skipper."

"It isn't?"

"You wanted to name him Captain, after that dog you lost," she said. "We compromised on Skipper."

How did she remember that? He didn't even remember it. Well, not exactly. But once she said it, Ira recalled the fight he'd had with Carol about the whole naming issue. As a child, he and Cliff had shared a black lab named Captain that had disappeared. For years, Ira kept an eye out for the dog, even when it was obvious to him that the dog was long since dead. Ira still looked every black lab over and tried to see if there was some glimmer of genetic recognition. "Is it you?" he'd whisper, and sometimes he thought he saw a familiar perk, a rise of the ears, a tilt of the head.

When he and Carol adopted their own dog, he told her the story of his missing pet and asked if it might be okay if they named their new dog Captain. She called him morbid and intimated he was stuck in the past and, upon current reflection, Ira saw the wisdom in both.

"I guess you were right about me being morbid back then," Ira said.

"There's no right or wrong about it, sweetheart," Carol said.

Skipper sat up and seemed lost for a moment, his eyes darting around the foyer without landing on anything in particular. Ira reached down and touched the dog's nose, a move that had always calmed Skipper, and the dog turned and greeted him with two happy yelps. For the last year, Ira sensed that Skipper was on the wrong end of a slippery slope and that each day they spent together should be memorable in some distinct way. Ira wasn't sure there was an afterlife for dogs, or people for that matter, but he reasoned that he'd better try his very best to cover his metaphysical bases, never mind the emotional ones.

"I don't know if I told you this," Ira said, "but I found out what happened to Captain. My dad called me last year and confessed that Captain was run over by a car. For an entire summer he let me and Cliff walk around the neighborhood knocking on doors asking people if they'd seen our dog. I bet half the neighborhood knew, right? I mean, what are the odds? Here I am forty-three years old and for the last thirty-five years I believed Captain just disappeared. Poof! Into the ether. Thirty-five years my mom and dad kept that from me. Can you believe that?"

A horn honked outside and Ira saw Carol frown.

"Skipper doesn't have much time left," Carol said.

"Don't say that."

"One of us has to," she said.

There were days when Ira was certain Carol hated him. The fact that she'd married Sayid so the he could return to the US legally played into this, and then the fact that she'd actually fallen in love with him and had gone on to have what appeared to be a solid and sustaining relationship didn't help, but Ira still felt like those things were done out of a desire for a substantial life and not to actually harm Ira. He didn't feel like today was one of the days when Carol actively wished him ill, and that made her proclamation all the sadder to him. He could see Skipper was old, could recognize the way Skipper's eyes had turned a milky blue, could smell a change in the dog's odor, an aroma that reminded him of his prized parcel of land, a smell that brought him to tears the first time he was able to accurately place it. Skipper was rotting from the inside.

"I'd like to keep him for the week," Ira said.

"That's fine." The horn honked again, this time for a solid five seconds. Carol wrapped her arms around herself and shivered. "You keep it so cold in here," she said.

Ira had long lost hope that they might reconcile, but that morning, as Carol stood and watched him pet their dog for several silent minutes, he felt a gap give way between them, as if all the years they'd known each other, all the wars they'd fought and lost together and apart, had finally left them in a position of casual peace, if only for the sake of their dog. Once Skipper was gone, Ira thought, there'd be nothing left to bind them.

"Do you remember how you once compared me to John Wayne?"

"I never did that," she said.

"You did," Ira said.

"I was probably just making conversation."

"It wasn't a positive thing," Ira said, and Carol seemed to glean some relief from that. "At the time, I kind of took it like it was, but it wasn't. I don't want to be John Wayne. John Wayne's dead. Just take a look around this fucking place."

The horn honked one more time, followed by the shrill ring of Carol's cell phone. "I have to go," Carol said. "Make some decisions about Skipper, okay?"

Ira watched from the closed-circuit TV in his office as Carol and Sayid wound their way out of WarTime, past the berms, sand dunes, and scorched skeletons of old cars. Just as his ex-wife and her husband pulled through the exit gate and hit the interstate, Ira saw Cliff rise up from a shallow bunker with a sword in one hand and a dead roadrunner in the other.

Ira buzzed his secretary. "Get my mother on the phone," he said, "and bring me Skipper's box of toys, please."

You only get so many chances to do the right thing, Ira thought. Here he was, an adult man in his early forties—God, when had that happened?—and his entire life had been lived in service to others. What had it earned him? He was wealthy beyond comprehension now, to the point that it would be literally impossible for him to spend all he'd earned in his lifetime, assuming he didn't purchase the Yankees. If he just lived like a normal rich person, the way his accountant figured it, Ira would have to live 179 more years to reach absolute zero. But as he walked Skipper along the shore of the Salton Sea, the sound of small arms fire echoing in the distance, Ira contemplated how little he enjoyed any of it. Life during WarTime sucked, there was no doubt about that, but it was the life he'd picked for himself and thousands of people daily garnered great joy from it. There had to be some small recompense in that.

Even still, Ira couldn't figure out why he'd been fixated on John Wayne so much lately, why he mentioned it to Carol. When he put his mind to it, he couldn't come up with a single John Wayne movie he'd actually enjoyed. In fact, his most enduring memory of Wayne was the actor's final appearance on the Academy Awards. He was frail from cancer and his face looked gaunt and...*disappeared*. Yes, Ira thought, *disappeared*. Already dead. The audience gave him a long ovation and all Ira could remember was that Wayne appeared scared, like he'd never before realized that eventually the applause would taper out, the people would file from the auditorium, and he'd know that they'd all said farewell to him before he was even gone. What a terrible fate: to out live your own death.

Maybe that was it. Maybe that's what it had always been.

Ira paused along the water's edge, removed Skipper's leash and let the dog meander a bit on his own. They were a safe distance away from any simulations and Ira knew that there was probably an Intelligence Advisor lurking about somewhere anyway, so it was safe to let the dog have some freedom. That night a group of retired Gulf War Generals were coming in for a live ammo reunion—they'd rented the whole park out for the evening—and this would probably be the last time Ira would feel secure walking along what would be the mouth of the Euphrates once his R & D people mocked it up. It would take weeks to clear the park of live rounds and booby traps and post-traumatics, but the vets paid big bucks and demanded reality.

Fuck reality. Who wanted it anymore? What everyone really wanted was the perception of reality, the idea of truth, not truth itself. The actuality of life was, as Ira's mother had said to him on the phone that morning, not all that encouraging. Especially as it related to Cliff. "Your brother always craved attention," she said. "You should have known that a little responsibility would drive him crazy."

"So this is my fault?"

"Why not have him arrested?"

"That's no solution," Ira said.

"You called and asked for my advice," she said. "I gave it."

They both stopped speaking for a moment and Ira could hear FoodTV running in the background at his mother's house. Rachel Ray was making Thanksgiving dinner in thirty minutes.

"Look," Ira said, "I'm thinking of selling WarTime, and I just want to get this Cliff issue worked out."

"Let him be," his mother said.

"Let him be? That's it?"

"Did he look happy when you saw him this morning?"

Ira rewound the tape of his brother and watched it again. He didn't look *unhappy*. In fact, Ira noticed that he'd lost about ten pounds and that the deep suntan he had made him look five years younger. The dead roadrunner in his hand didn't seem to be all that pleased by the situation, but Cliff himself possessed a serene quality that belied the fact that he'd likely lost his mind.

"So just let him be," Ira said to his mother and it felt, for the first time, like the proper course of action.

Now, as he watched Skipper sniff at a dead tilapia that had washed up onto the sand, he couldn't think of why he was so mad at Cliff in the first place. Surely his anger owed its luster to the past: The days and nights of his childhood spent searching for Captain. The end of his marriage, born out of benign neglect. The onset of inertia. It was all part of a greater ill, Ira was sure. He'd felt a twinge of sorrow in Carol when he saw her this morning and it took him all afternoon to figure out that it was pity; that his life, while rich, while obscene with materials, boiled down to a simple absurdity: at his lowest point last night, at three o'clock in the morning, he'd asked to see his dog.

Skipper scooped up the dead tilapia in his mouth, walked several steps into the Salton Sea, deposited the fish back into the water, and then turned and looked at Ira. He loved Skipper in an irrational way, he knew that. He'd even looked into getting him cloned at a laboratory in Sweden, had called Carol in the middle of the night and read her information he'd found on the lab's website that suggested dog cloning was only a few years away and with a donation of $100,000, Ira could ensure that Skipper would be one of the first. "Old animals die," Carol told him that night, "just like everything else."

"But he's young," Ira responded. "He's just a boy."

Every aspect of his life had taken on the caste of permanence, Ira realized, which was why WarTime was such a draw: Every battle could be refought, every loss avenged, every life preserved. Simulation was where the truth was. If only he could pay someone to simulate his life—even just the last twenty years would be fine.

Skipper kept his eyes locked on Ira's and took another step into the sea, and then another, and another, until the water lapped at his chin. I should find John Wayne and tell him that they were clapping for themselves, Ira thought; because they had survived, had stayed young, had not yet made the mistakes that lead to one final dirge of an ovation. Ira stepped into the water beside his dog and felt a wave of happiness pass through him. He touched Skipper's nose and it was warm and wet and though he could hear one of his Intelligence Advisors splashing into the water behind him, radioing into the base camp that the boss had gone "FUBAR, Code 9, FUBAR," Ira continued following his dog into the water, imagining all the while that he'd find John Wayne on the other side.

THE DISTANCE BETWEEN US

There's a cover band that plays each Tuesday night at the bar across the street from my apartment. I sit in my living room with the window open and listen, hoping that they'll play this Harry Chapin song my brother Lance used to listen to all the time. It was that one about the cab driver and his ex-girlfriend and…oh, it doesn't matter. They never play it anyway. No one ever does, I guess. Harry Chapin songs aren't that popular with the kids who go to bars on Tuesday nights.

My brother was an original. Not a fake bone in his body. God, he liked those artists who sang story songs: Gordon Lightfoot, Jim Croce, James Taylor—he even listened to Jimmy Buffett's boat songs. He said guys who sang songs about life were real and that bands like Styx and Journey were just "filler." He liked that word: filler.

"Don't buy that Camaro," he said to me once. I was sixteen and had worked all summer so that I could afford a beat-up Camaro that had mismatched rims and had been painted with primer and then never finished. "It's just filler. Save another two, three months and get something decent, dependable, like a Honda. Something that will last."

I drove that Camaro for three months before the transmission blew and the radiator cracked. I've got a Honda now, a real fancy Accord with a six CD changer and seventeen-inch tires, but I don't have my brother. He's been gone now for a year and while I don't mourn him every day, I do think about him and sometimes I talk to him about things that are bothering me. I'm not crazy, you know. I'm not conjuring his spirit and having talks with him and Houdini over the Ouija board. But like right now, with the band across the way playing this U2 song, I'm saying to Lance, "When are they going to learn some classics?" and he's saying, or I'm imagining he's saying, "You're right, Daryl. Why don't we go down there and request 'Please Come to Boston.' What do you say? I'll buy the first round."

I get up from my chair by the window and go to the fridge for two Rolling Rocks. One year he's been gone, I think, and I'm still drinking for two. Maybe I am crazy.

Mom and Dad show up at nine o'clock in the morning and buzz me from the street.

"We're double-parked," Dad says. "Just come on down and we'll take one car."

"I'm not ready yet," I say. "I just got out of the shower."

"Show some respect," Dad says. "Other people are waiting, too."

"I'll be down," I say. "Just give me a minute."

Dad makes a sound that I remember from my youth—it's something between a snort and a cough, and all it means is that words have failed him, that he's without an answer to anything.

I look outside and see Mom sitting in the front seat of Dad's old Lincoln Continental. She's wearing a hat today, the same wide-brimmed number she wore to Lance's funeral. I wonder if she even realizes it. Dad's pacing the sidewalk with his hands stuffed into the pockets of his suit coat, so that his arms look like bows.

You can't choose your parents and, even if you could, what difference would it make? Would they be any nicer? Would they love you any more or less? I was raised well, and though I never felt that I was as important to them as Lance, I realized that my parents loved me as much as they could. And that was fine. Lance was their first born, but he was also the dreamier one, prone to bouts of depression and anger, and while we rarely fought, he often would end up brawling with both Mom and Dad over the simplest things. The end result was that Lance had no ambition to go into business, had no desire to live his life in a suit and tie like our father; all he knew he was good at was drawing. Much of Mom and Dad's time was taken up worrying about Lance, wondering what he would make of his life, until he finally enlisted in the Marines. This was in 1990.

Lance found out then that, in addition to drawing, he also liked guns, and some recreational drugs. He served in Desert Storm and got used to having the chance to kill people. His friend Owen told me Lance probably killed fifty Iraqis, but Lance never really said anything about that. He did show me a charcoal drawing he made of the burning oil rigs in Kuwait. "See how I made the shadows and the smoke overlap? You see that?"

"Yeah," I said. "That makes it look real scary."

"No, no," Lance said. "That's the most peaceful thing. That's how it actually was. I could watch that smoke all day."

"What's this say in the corner?" I asked. There was a signature there, but it wasn't Lance's.

"That's my artist name," he said. "Honeymoon Lewis. What do you think?"

"Sounds a little goofy," I said.

Lance smiled real big and then slapped at my face gently. "That's right! You got it," he said. "Like somebody in a story, right? Like somebody in a Harry Chapin song. Right?"

Mom looks up and sees me in the window. I smile and wave, but she doesn't move. So much of her life has been ruled by sorrow. What I perceive to be the truth of her life is that she wanted something more, something lucrative and deep that would have made her famous, would have put her in a spotlight where she could have been absolutely unique. Maybe she would have danced with Nureyev or perhaps she would have gone up in the space shuttle. There was always something she wanted to do.

We'd go to the library when I was a kid, and she'd check out books about science and horticulture, and sometimes she'd get these thick tomes about metaphysics and past-life regression. More often than not, Mom would read these books in a day or two and then she'd sit in the living room making lists and charts and diagrams about…about…God, I have no idea what they were about! I'd try and catch a peek at her work, and she'd snatch the paper up and tear it to pieces. In my mind, she was planning to change the world, was getting close to a fabulous universal truth, and then I'd come up behind her and she'd just crumple it up.

Though I suppose the profundity of this truth could be wrong: she is just a woman who gave birth to two sons, one of whom decided to kill a cop a year ago today.

Dad drives with his window down so that the smoke from his cigar doesn't bother Mom and me. It's pointless, though: the one person who should be bothered, the one who had his cancerous left lung carved out of his chest two years ago, is the one smoking the toxic thing.

"You should really quit smoking," I say. "It's harmful to all of us."

"All bets are off." Dad smiles at me in the rearview mirror. "These are my bonus years. I should already be gone. I'm allowed to celebrate."

"That's so illogical," Mom says. "Do you even hear yourself?"

"Loud and clear," he says.

When we were kids, Dad used to give Lance and me his old cigar boxes. We'd fill them with matchbox cars or army men, or sometimes we'd just leave them empty so that we could smell the sweet tobacco when Dad was at work. Dad also thought one day they might be worth something, like the baseball cards he'd thrown away as a kid.

"Do you still have any old cigar boxes?" I ask.

"No," Dad says. "Threw them all out. They're not worth a damn cent, you know. Saw something on PBS about it. Not a damn cent."

"Still," I say, "it would be neat to have a few of them."

"It would, Daryl," Dad says, and then I see him pat Mom lightly on the thigh. "Maybe we'll hit some garage sales one of these days, see what we find. How does that sound?"

A convertible Mustang filled with teenage girls speeds past us, and I think that if Lance were here right now he'd tell me that Dad was trying and that I should respond to him, that Dad needs to be commended when he does something right. "Yes," I say. "That would be fun."

After Desert Storm, Lance came home with a bitterness I'd never seen before. He said he'd done things he didn't like to hold himself accountable for and that no matter what else happened to him for the rest of his life, he'd understand that he was just a vessel. He actually said that. We we're sitting at T.G.I. Friday's eating potato skins and drinking Mudslides and he said, "You ever feel like a vessel?"

"I don't think I know what you mean," I said.

"Yes you do," he said. "Like you're not in control. Like someone else is pulling all the strings and you're just performing a task."

"No," I said.

"My wiring is all screwed up," he said. "I've got a whole jumble of things acting inside me and I'm just, you know, doing time in my body."

"Lance," I said, "you okay?"

He picked up a potato skin and took a deep bite into it. "I've been craving one of these for over a year," he said. "You'd be amazed by the things you think about in the middle of a desert. T.G.I. Friday's potato skins and Mudslides seemed to pop up quite a bit."

After we drank another three Mudslides, Lance got up and said he was going to step outside for some fresh air and would be right back. For two hours I waited for him. I checked the bathroom, the bar, the parking lot. I asked if anyone had noticed him walking around. Nothing. It was like he just vanished into the ether. Though we were both pretty drunk, it wasn't like Lance to walk out of a place without saying anything. He just wasn't like that. I didn't see him again for two years.

Mom flips on the radio and Al Green's voice fills the car. He's singing "Let's Stay Together," and for a while no one says anything.

Lance loved Al Green. Said he was the last man on earth who knew what true love was. Lance said things like that.

"You know he's a preacher now," Dad says. "Al Green, I mean."

"I heard that," I say.

We are a few miles from the cemetery and already I feel like jumping out of the car and running home. It's not the knowledge that I'm going to visit my dead brother, because I do that often, but that I know what we'll find once when we get there: someone defaces his tombstone at least once a week. There's usually something like COP KILLER written over his name. I've found dead rats, skunks, human waste, all manner of disgusting items strewn over Lance's grave.

He was my brother. I'm not sorry about that.

What am I supposed to feel? Am I supposed to admit that my brother was the most evil monster who ever lived? Chances are, there are people who would want me to say that Lance deserved to die, that he was a mistake of society, but the truth is that I never knew that side of him, never knew he killed a prostitute in Laughlin, Nevada, years before he killed a police officer here in town, or that he was even capable of either.

All of that sounds like filler to me. I've been on this planet for thirty years, and while I know that doesn't qualify me as an expert on this existence, I believe you can love someone and never really know their deepest secrets or begin to understand what drives them to madness. There are places you just don't go with people you care about, family or otherwise.

After he disappeared from T.G.I. Friday's, Lance drifted up to Laughlin and got a job drawing caricatures in the lobby of a casino. He'd left a note on Mom and Dad's kitchen table telling them he was going away, but not to worry. He eventually called me after he'd been up there for about six months and apologized for just disappearing.

"Tell Mom and Dad that it felt too weird being back home," he said. "I didn't want to see anyone I knew from high school and have them ask me what I was doing. What do you say? I just got back from killing some towelheads, how about you? You know what I mean, right Daryl?"

"You could have stayed with me," I said. "Just hung out for a week or two until you got back to feeling normal again."

Lance didn't say anything for a moment. "I couldn't do that to you," he said softly. "You're a good kid, Daryl. Maybe you'll come up and see me sometime? We'll hit the casinos, maybe rent a couple jet skis and pick up girls on the river. We'd have a good time."

"I'd like that," I said.

"I'm gonna send you a couple of my new drawings," Lance said before we hung up. "I feel like I'm doing some really good work out here."

A few days later, a thick manila envelope arrived at my apartment, filled with caricatures, landscapes, and abstract drawings—along with Polaroid pictures of what Lance was trying to capture. He had a clean and oddly effortless way with people's faces, somehow coaxing humanity out of black lines of ink, and showed an especially flawless knack for children.

As I sifted through the Polaroids, comparing them to the drawings, I came across a photo that had no corresponding art work. A young woman in a bathing suit was sitting on a chaise lounge reading a magazine, her eyes shielded by sunglasses. She seemed oblivious to the fact that someone was taking pictures of her. When I called Lance to thank him for sending me his work, I asked him about the girl.

"She's a friend," he said. "I didn't mean to send that to you."

"Are you drawing her?"

"No," Lance said.

"You should," I said. "She's gorgeous. Do you want me to send it back?"

"Don't worry about it," he said. "Keep everything or throw it out. I don't care."

"Are you all right?" I asked. There was something in Lance's voice that made me think he was in a hurry, a sense that he wasn't really paying attention to anything I was saying.

"I'm late for work," Lance said. "I just have to get down to the casino."

"Maybe I'll come up next week," I said. "I've got a few vacation days left that I can use."

"That won't work for me," Lance said. "Maybe next month? Definitely come up next month."

After we hung up, I sat for a long time and looked at Lance's drawings. I noticed that he'd signed each of them, but not with his own name. Instead, in his perfect cursive, he'd written "Art by Honeymoon Lewis" in the corner of each.

Mom turns around in her seat and smiles at me. "We haven't really talked," she says. "How is everything going?"

"I'm fine," I say. We've pulled into the cemetery grounds and are winding through the soft foothills filled with headstones. I've always thought that cemeteries were a waste—a place you visit just to feel awful, a place that shows the determined end of everything. No matter the trials or tribulations or the defining variables of your life, the conclusion is the same. But I continue to visit because I know that beneath my feet is something that was once my brother.

"It would be nice if you came by every now and then," Mom says. "I feel like I never get to see you."

"I should get you email," I say. "It's the best way to get a hold of me."

"I don't understand how you can spend so much time staring at a computer," Mom says. I design websites for a living—and that's just what it is: a living. "Do you like your job?"

"It's what I've chosen to do," I say.

"You know what I mean, Daryl," she says. "Does it make you happy? Are you fulfilled?"

There is not a correct set of answers for these questions. Dad always wanted me, like Lance years before, to go into "business"—meaning something that involved the law or balance sheets or stocks. For years, Dad was a partner in a small law firm specializing in bankruptcy, a decidedly unglamorous field of law, and had long hoped that either Lance or I would follow the same path and that we'd open a family practice. Mom only desired that we do what we wanted, and that we had no misgivings about our choices.

"I'm happy," I say. "The job itself doesn't give me great joy, but the money is good and I have free time to do what I want when I get home. It keeps me busy."

"You should make time for a family," Dad says, the first time he's spoken in several minutes.

"He's right," Mom says.

"Maybe I'll do that," I say. "Do you know where I can sign up for something like that?"

"We're being serious," Mom says. "You don't want to live your life with any regrets about things you could have done. End up in a place like this because you've run out of options."

"That's not why Lance is dead," I say.

"That's enough," Dad says. "I don't want to talk about it. Not today."

"Then when?" I ask.

"Daryl," Mom says, "let's just remember the good parts of Lance right now. Make it easier on all of us."

"You can't run away from the truth forever," I say. "You can't just try to rationalize the fact that Lance wasn't the person you thought he was. When are either of you going to admit that?"

"Not today!" Dad shouts and then turns up the radio, filling the car with music. It doesn't come close to drowning out the sounds of Mom's crying.

Lance started getting in trouble in Laughlin. Twice he was picked up for buying drugs—coke both times—and once on suspicion of robbery, but nothing stuck until he busted up a tourist inside the casino. He called me from county jail and said he'd beaten up a man he was drawing a caricature of. The man had complained that the drawing looked nothing like him, that he certainly did not have a double chin or long black hairs hanging from his nose, but Lance told him he was just drawing what he saw. When the man refused to pay, Lance severely thumped him with his fold-up easel.

"How much is bail?" I asked.

"No," he said, "don't worry about that. I go to court in the morning and then I'll get released. I just wanted you to know where I was."

"I'll be there in four hours," I said.

"You're a good kid," Lance said.

After I posted his bail, Lance came out of the jail and hugged me in the lobby. He seemed taller than when I'd last seen him at T.G.I. Friday's; his skin stretched tight over his face and hands. It gave me the impression that he was somehow growing, that his bones would eventually punch through his skin. I thought then that he might just extend beyond my reach, that he'd slide past me into the sky.

He'd lost weight, nearly twenty pounds by my guess, and his hair was long and greasy. We walked across the street to a crowded diner, one of those places with a checkerboard floor where the waiters dressed like soda jerks, and ordered cheeseburgers.

"You've gotta understand something about drawing for these fucking people," Lance said. We were sitting in a booth, eating dinner, and Lance was starting to get loud. "There's a certain amount of stupidity you've gotta deal with. That's fine. I can do that. I was a Marine, you know? But you get some poor fucker from Nebraska who wants a fucking portrait of himself to take back to his fat ass wife back home, a fucking keepsake, and he says, you know, make it look real, like I don't know my fucking job. And so I give him real. I give him two-fucking-dimensions of real. I put my fucking heart and soul into that fucking pen. And you know what he says? You know what this fucking fuck says? He says it doesn't look like how he wants it to look! So I say lose some fucking weight, you know? Daryl, this guy had it coming like no one has ever had it coming."

Lance never swore—he always said that there were thousands of words better than a curse. He told me once—this was when I was ten and had just gone 0-4 in a Little League game and was trying out all the four letter words I'd ever heard—that swearing was a sign of weakness, a display of caving in.

"Lance," I said. "Calm down. You're making a scene. There are kids here."

"It's Honeymoon," he said. "Okay? Lance is dead and gone. From here on out I am Honeymoon. And tell Mom and Dad that, too. I don't want birthday cards or Christmas gifts addressed to that son of a bitch Lance."

"Are you on something?"

Lance stared at me from across the table and I could have sworn it was a complete stranger, an alien inside my brother's body. Then his face softened, his eyes closed, and he took several deep breaths, almost as if he'd just come up from being underwater. "I'm sorry," he said. "You drove all the way up here to get me out of a tight spot and here I am acting crazy. You shouldn't have to see me like this—it's not your fault. Christ, it's not your fault at all."

Lance ended up doing sixty days, got fired from his job, got another on a riverboat, and then rather suddenly picked up and moved to Biloxi, where he ended up getting married, having a kid, and getting a divorce all within the space of two years. He called me the day the divorce was finalized.

"You should fly out here," he said. "James Taylor is playing an outdoor concert next week, and I've got a buddy who can get us some good seats. Maybe even backstage passes. It would be a real fun time. You could meet your niece, Carol Ann, too. She'd love to meet you, Daryl. God, it would be great if you could fly out. What do you think?"

"I'd like to," I said, "but I can't just pick up and leave work. Maybe if we could plan something in advance I could get time off."

"I understand," Lance said. "Hell, I could probably use a little of that structure back in my life."

"Are you working?"

"I've got my own stand out in the arts district," he said. "I'm making enough to live on, you know, but Shelly's got me bent over backwards now." Shelly was his ex-wife.

"Why don't you come back out here?" I said. "Until you can get back on your feet."

"Maybe I will," he said. "We could have a good time together, don't you think? Maybe get a place where you could put my drawings on the Internet. I could become rich and famous."

The next time I saw Lance was on the television. He was standing in front of a McDonald's here in town with a gun pointed at a cop's head. Fifteen minutes later, as I sat riveted to the TV, screaming, crying, begging for something, anything, to happen to save Lance, my older brother shot the policeman. Half a second later, Lance was dead, too. The coroner said to the press that he was shot thirty-six times, but that with the amount of PCP he had in his system, it was probably—"unfortunately," he said—a painless death.

I spray Lance's tombstone with 409 and get to work on the graffiti. Dad picks up scraps of garbage and old vegetables and tucks them into a sack. Mom stands unmoving a few yards away, her arms crossed over her chest. It's harder for her, I think, because Lance was a physical part of her for nine months, a part of her that has become wretched with decay, torn by the memory of a newscast she witnessed just like everybody else.

As I scrub, I start to talk to Lance. I tell him that today has been pretty tough, that Mom and Dad just aren't in tune, and that Al Green was on the radio when we pulled up. I tell him I think hearing "Let's Stay Together" was an omen, that he was looking down on us and telling us to get along. And then I say, God dammit, Lance. Why did you go crazy? Why did you hurt people? Why didn't you just come here like we talked about, hang with me for a little while, concentrate on your art? Why did you kill a woman in Laughlin, Nevada? Why did you send me her picture? Did you want to get caught? And then I say, I miss you, Lance. I miss talking about cars and music and about how if you had a choice you'd just draw all day, never even sleep or eat. I remind Lance about the night we got into a fight at a bar with a guy who said Elton John could kick Billy Joel's ass and then, later, all three of us ended up singing terrible karaoke versions of both of their hits. I start to laugh and then I look up and see that my Dad has stopped picking up trash and is just looking at me with this completely lost expression on his face.

"Do you remember how Lance used to listen to those story-songs?" I ask.

"I do," Dad says, and then he starts laughing, too. "He used to turn up the volume so loud that the neighbors would complain, and Lance would say, 'How can you complain about a Loggins & Messina song?'"

"What was he like as a baby?"

"He was just a kid, Daryl." Dad shrugs. "If you're asking if there were signs, things we should have looked out for, well, that I don't know. Maybe your mother does."

Mom has stepped away from us and is walking slowly along the gravel path that surrounds the rows of graves.

"You haven't talked about it?"

"Of course we have," he says. "There are distances between everyone, Daryl. We have ours, too."

Down the hill from us, a group of kids has gathered around a grave. They are all wearing football jerseys, and after a few moments they break into song. It wafts up in the air, and for a moment Dad and I stop cleaning and just listen.

"So much sorrow here," Dad says, and then he touches me lightly on the arm. It feels warm, and I wonder how long it has been since we've hugged. A year, I think. Maybe more.

"Did you ever think this could happen?" I say.

"How do you prevent the unimaginable? How do you teach your son not to be a serial killer, Daryl?" Dad says. "I wish someone could tell me."

"I miss him," I say.

"So do I," Dad says, and then we get back to cleaning Lance's grave so Mom can have her time alone with him.

The police scoured every piece of Lance's life. They trundled through his apartment in Biloxi, through his belongings stored at Mom and Dad's house, through the photos and art he'd given me, and put together the picture of a man I did not know. They were certain he'd killed the woman in the Polaroid—a prostitute who often stayed in the hotel Lance worked at—and were under the assumption he'd killed another two women in Mississippi. There were drawings.

Lance's ex-wife, Shelly, didn't come down for the funeral. She said she didn't want to put herself and Carol Ann through that sort of spectacle. She'd rather remember him as a human, not an atrocity. And those were her exact words. Two weeks later, she flew into town with some of Lance's belongings, and so Mom and Dad could meet Carol Ann.

"These are all his records," Shelly said. We were standing outside my apartment unloading boxes from the trunk of Dad's car. Shelly was a pretty girl, not even twenty-one then, but time and circumstance had already begun to weigh on her. I thought that when I was twenty-one, eight years earlier, I still felt like a kid, still wondered when I was going to become an adult. There was an eternity about things then, but Shelly had needed to become an adult in an instant, and I felt sorry for that.

"You should keep these," I said. "He'd probably be happy to know you were listening to them."

"I don't want them in my home," Shelly said. "I hear him in every song, and I can't live like that."

That night, I sat on the floor for hours playing old LPs, cassette tapes, and CDs. I listened to Harry Chapin and Jim Croce, Neil Young and John Denver, Al Green and Otis Redding. I listened to every song I thought Lance loved until they all started to sound the same, until the sun was rising and I was drunk and crying and wondering how you lose sight of the people who mean something to you.

The days unwind like an old alarm clock. I wake up. I go to work. I eat. I drink. I talk to my dead brother until I think I can hear him in the grooves of his old records, until I am clear that none of what existed in him exists in me.

I go to a pottery class with my mother. I go to garage sales with my dad, and together we search for a cigar box that will mean something to us. We buy hundreds and none of them do the trick. I enjoy our time together, but think that in some strange way Dad feels he's paying a tithe for a life he might have otherwise given up on—his and mine.

And still.

Honeymoon Lewis arrives via UPS and stares down at me from the wall. Shelly calls to make sure the painting has arrived safely, to make sure the police sent it to where she specified. He stands barefoot on the hardwood in the kitchen of our childhood home. He has a strong jaw, dark blue eyes, and wispy brown hair. It is Lance's finest work—a self-portrait of man who never existed, a dream for time and hope. It is familiar and haunting, yet when all the familiars pass away, when I stare at the painting for hours imagining Lance at work, all that is left are his strokes with a paintbrush, his finetuned hand on canvas, his every movement another story, another song, another ending.

ACKNOWLEDGMENTS

This collection represents several years of writing—from a time in my life when I wondered if anyone would ever read my words, to a time when it became clear that words were now my career—and I would be remiss if I did not thank the many people whose hands touched these tales. It is with deep gratitude that I thank Mary Yukari Waters, Noah Nussbaum, Nancy Matson, Teresa Burkett, Kim Wildman, Vincent Precht, Jane Lukes, Tom Stringer, Dantae Davies, Shirley Asano Guldimann, Gary Glickman and Diane Lefer for their astute criticism regarding many of my early stories, and for their patience. Thanks are also due to Jack Lopez for giving me inspiration long before any dreams were fulfilled and for introducing me to short fiction that challenged me. I'm ever grateful to my literary agents, Jennie Dunham, for her keen eye, insight, and unwavering belief in my work, and Judi Farkas, for her continued enthusiasm and zest for my fiction.

It has been such a pleasure working with the good people of *Other Voices*/OV Books and I am honored to be the author of their first book. My relationship with *Other Voices* magazine began many years ago when Founding Editor Lois Hauselman agreed to publish the title story of this collection, and has continued through my long friendship with Gina Frangello, perhaps the sharpest and most skilled editor I've had the pleasure of working with. I am humbled by the attention and skill given to this manuscript by the entire *Other Voices* team, including Allison Parker, JoAnne Ruvoli, Stacy Bierlein, Amy Davis and Matt Pagano.

None of this would have been possible without the support and encouragement of my family, friends, editors, employers and

booksellers across the country—in particular, my brother Lee
Goldberg, Todd Harris, Jim Kochel, Steve Nitch, Scott Phillips,
Peter Handel, AJ & Brenda Holcomb, Geoff Schumacher, Andrew
Kiraly, Kristin Petersen, Linda Venis and the UCLA Extension
Writers' Program, Sheldon MacArthur and the Mystery Bookstore,
Lita Weissman, Kris Darnall and Nevada Humanities, Angela Park
and the Environmental Leadership Program, my students and the
fine literary journals who first published these stories.

And, finally, Wendy, who believed before anyone.